K-9 4.95

The Dweller on the Threshold

The Dweller on the Threshold

Patricia Joudry

McClelland and Stewart Limited

0-7710-4466-6

The Canadian Publishers
McClelland and Stewart Limited
25 Hollinger Road, Toronto

PRINTED AND BOUND IN CANADA

The poem on page 105 is reprinted
by permission of Peter Viereck
from his collection *New and Selected Poems.*

For my parents,
Beth and Clifford Joudry,
with love

Year One

I can barely remember the journey. As though in a dream or by thought alone, I have travelled the distance and the years, and stand with the sea at my back looking up at the house where I was born. It hugs the high slope above the water as firmly as it did in my boyhood, despite the networks of caves far below, slowly corroding the rock on which it stands.

My father, who never boasted, boasted only of this, that our setting was individual, unique on this wooded Canadian Pacific coast. The one spearhead of rock was perhaps thrown down at the cooling of the earth by the distant mountain rising blue above the chimney pots. The trees around the house are few but strong, for their roots are sunk in rock; their numbers gradually increase as the earth takes up again on either side. To my right the rain forest crowds the water, leaving only a narrow strip of beach. On my left is the high grassy headland.

I climb the tangled terraces which once were lawns, studying the scene with new eyes and a great sense of removal. Woehill House. The hill is here, rising behind the house and slanting north toward the headland, leading steeply to the jagged pines that separate it from the sky; the woe has been here but has gone, and it was not the most of it.

The place has the feel of autumn and the look of spring. There is death in the air, in the taste of my mouth and the look of the abandoned house. Yet the roses are growing all over it like beauty gone crazy. Their trellises must have rotted long ago, and the vines are without direction, but strong with the strength of freedom. They are spreading everywhere, in wild bursts of energy, stringing themselves across windows and doors and emblazoning the chimneys with scarlet and green as though decorating them for Christmas. It seems that only the hardiest life can endure here, and it is invincible.

The roses make the house look cohesive at last. It was built in a dozen different styles by my great-great grandfather, who fled England and a domestic scandal only to start another one here . . . or so it was designated by his New World offspring. He fell under the spell of an Iroquois maid and raised these roofs in her honour, choosing the best features of every English house he had ever seen. He used granite for endurance and stained glass for fun. Its gables put the house of seven in the shade. The ground floor windows touch the ceiling, and the upper ones are round and small, like a pack of one-eyed sailors squinting out to sea. Every room had a fireplace, and though most have been replaced by modern heating the chimney pots remain; for there was a superstitious fear in our family that any disturbance of the weird and delicate balance might crash the whole thing to the ground.

All this the Great-great crowned with a small watch-tower, commemorating perhaps his early years on the sea and his escape across it. The hours I spent up there remain the purest and clearest of my life, and hover even now above my head, luminous and timeless and apart from the phantom feeling around me. The roses have not yet reached the tower, though a stiff tendril is pointing determinedly upward from a west attic dormer.

There's no sound from the caves below. The tide is out and the air perfectly still. It was the whine of wind in the caves that made the eerie music she and I used to love, as we lay flat, pressing an ear to the grass. Or at high tide, the lick of greedy waters used to thrill us also – until a certain day.

I am going to have to go in. There's an inventory to do, and everything will have to be disposed of. I have known that the day would come. . . . But the sea is so silent behind me, and the house as I draw near holds something of the same deep, awesome stillness. The roses look nightmarish now. And the front door, all pink and white and crimson, reminds me of a coffin banked with flowers, their explosive life underscoring the death within. The dead air inside the house takes on a substance: I feel it, like a presence, something waiting.

Before going in, I'll just walk around the house. ("Walk around me once for luck," she used to say.) I'll have to see to the condition of the grounds, in any case. Hard to believe this was the terrace. The flags must have split apart from the tough grass: killing grass we called it and we fought it. Now it has won.

("But dare not walk around me twice.")

I could look in a window. The furniture will all be there, unless vandals have been around. If it's been emptied, so much the easier.

Let's see the living room. I should have sold the Oriental carpets years ago. ("Look to the East, out the West window.") Strange fear, to look through a space in the roses. Rub the mist from the window . . . and there it is, the tall arched doorway from the hall, where she first appeared, so small, so prominent in her bright red dress. It shocked me; I'd expected her to be in black.

And there am I – sitting up slowly on the chesterfield, where I'd been dozing over *Heart of Darkness*. (We hadn't got to the darkness yet, it was all promises, promises, I longed for the heart of the thing.)

I stood up and said, "Are you. . . . "

"Yes!" she said.

" . . . Cecilia?" I couldn't believe it; all in possession of herself, with bright cheeks and sharp musical voice.

"I *said* I was Cecilia!" She marched past me across the room and looked around. No black on her anywhere except her hair, which fell straight down her back, as her back rose straight to meet it.

She said, "So this is your house."

"It . . . " I hear my voice, hesitant and already nervous with her, "it's your house now too. . . . "

"It's not my house! My house is in New York! I'm going back there someday to go on the stage. How can you stand it here?" She looked toward the windows, which were standing open to the sea. "Miles from anywhere." And I looked with her at the sea – past the man with full eyes looking in – and saw that it wasn't still that day, but tumultuous, ice green, with its dark heart deeply hidden. I had always thought of the sea as female, though it bore no comparison with my mother, who was simple, transparent and good. She had stitched by hand the white curtains at the window and every day arranged the bowls of roses which stood around on the tables among my father's many books.

I couldn't imagine any place nicer, but I said to Cecilia, "It's nicer outside. Would you like to go down to the beach?"

"No I wouldn't. The sand would ruin my shoes."

I looked at her shoes. They were white, and so brightly gleaming she might have been standing in two pools of light. She wore silk stockings on her thin little legs. Only her legs looked in the least way orphaned. Nothing else about her suggested that her mother had swallowed a bottle of pills the week before, after being attacked by a group of men called First Night Critics. It seemed, as far as I could make out from my parents' conversation, that they had not liked the way she acted. Her father was divorced from her mother, and anyway he was dead.

In two months she would be my age, thirteen, but she was much smaller and more drastically alive. I felt childish in her presence: reduced by the enormity of her experience.

"You could take your shoes off," I said respectfully, "and your stockings. Have you got a bathing suit?"

"I loathe swimming." Her voice was dramatic, very American. She began wandering around the room looking at pictures. "Are any of these originals?"

"That one is." I pointed. She looked at it with interest. "It's mine." She turned her back on it. It crossed my mind that she hated me. Perhaps it was because we were relatives; my mother and her mother were cousins.

There was something unpleasant to get over, and the longer I put it off ... "I'm awfully sorry ... " I said, starting over to her.

"You don't have to be!" she interrupted, with a sudden bright laugh. "Some people paint worse pictures than that. You should hear some of the critics ... " She broke off, and all the mourning that was absent from her clothes rushed into two half circles under her eyes. I felt I had to do something quickly. I leaned forward and kissed her on the cheek.

Then my own cheek sizzled. She had slapped me. It was the first slap I'd had in my life. I stared in astonishment.

"What did you do that for?"

"Oh I'm sorry, I'm terribly terribly sorry!" She took my hands and the tears she had been refusing rose into her eyes, blue eyes, blue and dark, almost black. I understood, and felt a rush of ease. For the first time I perceived the existence of dimensions other than the obvious. I sensed in a flash that the things we see, and the facts we think we know, are only tiny pinpoints on the surface of some deep, vast, hidden Otherness; and it is the Otherness that moves us.

"It's my temper," she said. "I have a dramatic temper'-ment. And besides, I'm a Scorpio." She turned and ran out of the room, her black hair flying like a wild silk flag.

I had never heard of a Scorpio. I opened the dictionary (on the long table by the window, here before my eyes) and, passing over "the eighth sign of the zodiac" which I did not understand, read with some foreboding of the creature with a long narrow tail terminating in a venomous sting.

I turn around and face the sea and its silence. Grey, and a grey sky, with a white sun burning behind it. The sea is quiet only because it's so far away – a low spring tide. Otherwise it's what it has always been. There is a certain character which never changes, though it effects radical alterations all around.

("*Yet if thou walkest round me thrice, I'll marry thee!*")

I start away toward the left corner of the house – then stop. There will be only space around the back where the coach house used to be; a jumble of roots like these under my feet. To walk across that space, even to see it . . .

The stone is mossed over, I see, beneath the vines. Damp probably, right through. I wouldn't give a nickel for the place myself. But what it must have cost to put it up! Who now would carve the gingerbread around the windows . . . and who would want it? ("When craftsmanship" . . . my father . . . "goes out of a society, the society soon follows.") I can see without looking the brass strips and scallops around the cupola at the top of the tower. The brass is that beautiful green that used to make Mathilde yearn to clean it. But it couldn't be reached. And no one could reach it from inside either, when you got up there and pulled the little stairs up after you. That's why we loved it. Squeezed together side by side (it was built only for one); dusk – our favourite time; the lighthouse flashing, pausing, flashing, far far out, and the stars beginning one by one above us and very close.

And other sights. Rain over the water, the foam rising to meet it, mingling with it in the air . . . fog rolling in off the sea, a soft wall advancing, creeping in among the firs, taking big quiet bites out of them . . . sunsets seen from the edge of night . . . and the Orient just over the watery hill. How many on earth can look to the East out a West window?

What did my Great-great see from it, standing with his back to England and tradition? Did he see that he would found a tradition of his own? He had been one of many and had separated and become many again. Dead and perfected, he gazed down upon our heads from his frame in the front hall, keeping his secrets . . . and one of our own. No one ever detected the little smudge between his eyebrows, that was not put there by the painter but by Cecilia's slingshot, loaded with turkish delight. The sticky impress very gradually collected dust, until we were certain it would be discovered.

"Anyway it improves him," she said. "He looks like a swami with an ash mark."

"What do they wear that for?"

"That's protection against evil, didn't you know?"

The Great-great's given name was Hedleigh. It had been his grandfather's before him, skip one, for it was handed out every second generation to avoid confusion within the family. That's how I had the bad luck for it to land on me. I would have liked to have been called Bob.

The name of his dark consort I never knew. She was not

mentioned. I referred to the heritage now and then for the reaction.

"After all, Mathilde, I *am* part Indian."

"You are never such a thing! One of your ancestors made once a terrible mistake, that is all! You are an Englishman!"

But I knew what I was. I was Canadian. I had my own ideas about what that meant, and I kept them to myself.

The Indian point, I knew better than to argue. The stigma was fading out, along with the pigment in skin and hair; for it became an unspoken point of honour in our family to marry blonds. I deduced this, anyway, looking through the albums. And the strain was settled firmly on its feet by my grandmother, my father's mother, who was not only pale-haired but born in Buckinghamshire. She sent my father over to Oxford to be educated, and he showed his thanks by coming back and marrying an American. However, my mother was from Boston and had an English accent almost as good as his, broader on "pyjamas," so it all worked out.

But I'll have to fight these people; they're trying to draw me back. I won't go inside a while yet; they'd score. ("HE SCORES!!!!" Foster Hewitt, Saturday night hockey, my father by the radio leaping two feet in his chair, the only times in his life when emotion ruled him . . .) I'll go down closer to the water.

The curve of the horizon is absolutely as it was. Time might have been standing still. Or curving perhaps, like that, a long slow curve . . . time as a curve, time a circle, a circle full of movement and feeling but forever fixed in its place . . . like a world – or a man. A man is a whole world: his belt goes around his equator, his heart radiates warmth, and his brain casts a chill from the North. But often his Eastern hand doesn't know what his West is doing. And if he stands with them both outstretched, he becomes a cross.

I sit down on a hummock, facing the sea. The still water

calms my mind. Thought ceases; I gaze into space, the infinitely extending waters, the simplicity of the great complex sky.

And then, so simply, almost as though nothing at all has happened, my years at this place present themselves to me whole. I see them in one piece, as though a light had flashed on inside a room, revealing everything at once; yet a certain distance remains between things.

Here we stand, still and in a thousand gestures, one gesture leading inevitably to the next, and the end contained in the beginning. Causes and effects are not separated; our suffering and our laughter are one event. My mother's tears flow steadily behind a smiling face like rain beyond a glass. My father, studious and serene, the embodiment of all the old Greek virtues, evokes an image of learning sunk at sea and knowledge dredged up, passing and surpassing. Mathilde, servant and despot, bows before her altar and before her stove, for they are one and the same.

I see the seasons overlaid, snow falling through the bright spring blossoms already turned to fruit, while autumn leaves fly upward in the sun and wind.

Moments, individual, but one with it all, emerge, hang in light, like the flowers on a particular boiling day in summer, looking as though they were melting around the edges. A day so hot that Mathilde was not cooking; and the sea looked like lava as I raced toward it. I tore into it and it socked me. I leaped about, yelling and shrieking, throwing up my arms then my rump to the sun.

At the same time I stood quietly by the edge of the water in the very early morning, the air oyster-grey with lavender shadows, and a full moon sailing low over the sea, past purple clouds hanging still. I stood in wonder on the shore and felt the living presence all around. It was more alive than I, and I wondered when, if ever, it would enter into me.

17

Yet I see, if I didn't then, that it was in me already, for I was made up of it. This I had not grasped, though I often pondered Plato's "Idea," the originating impulse in people and things which he considered their Reality.

Cecilia knew all about the Idea, for she lived it, and was furious when I tried to explain.

"You're ruining everything! Don't you know that as soon as you explain something it runs and hides? Explain the wind, and listen – the wind stops!"

"Well, I sure wish I could explain you."

"What?" . . . laughing . . . "and make me go away?"

"No . . . not that."

But that was later.

Or does later exist, and before? I could almost believe that sequence is an illusion; that everything happens all at once, in one infinite moment; or at least that wholeness and sequence co-exist. My life invites me to retrace it, and suggests it was already complete before I traced it.

Destiny, Cecilia explained when we were older, is like being on a journey along a road you've never travelled. But the road ahead is there, and the destination too.

And my career, was it written? What a fuss we might have saved . . .

"Teaching is an honourable profession, Hedleigh." My father had given it up with honour when he inherited Woehill House. "One of the noblest, if not the very noblest." And with his historical essays he made noble the name Gerald Gilbart.

Our own history I see through a slowly falling shower of fragments . . . Cecilia was rambunctious; she broke things.

"They're only things . . . " my father's voice; the sorrow in it and in my mother's face as their treasured past fell to pieces.

And in my ears is the splitting sound of the moments when the first great cracks appeared.

"What are you going to do when you grow up?"

The question came suddenly. We were walking home from school, the village school which I attended as a socializing measure only; for my real lessons were with my father.

"I'm going to teach History," I said. And I was being tutored by his great friend and former professor at Oxford, Professor Kingsford, who now lived near us.

"Why?"

The bare question, as we too were barefooted, poking our way along the sand.

"Because – well it's what I've always been going to do."

She was silent, but the sea set up a tumult beside me. I looked her way, and she was looking at me.

"History," she said, "has happened. Everybody knows about it. Why don't you teach something people don't know about yet?"

"How would I find it out?"

"If it was me," she said, "I'd find it."

"But how?"

"Never mind, it isn't me. I'm not going to teach, I'm going to learn."

"Learn what?"

"Everything!"

She wasn't going to learn that from Miss Platchett, whose life she made a misery, challenging and arguing. Not that she was rude. She would simply stand and ask one question, and the question would set off a chain of giggles along the desks because there was no answer to it, or if there was Miss Platchett didn't know it and never would.

"Your trouble," I told her, "is that you're conceited."

"I'm not!" She turned on me furiously. "I'm very hum-

19

ble! I want to know things. I have *nothing* . . . " she struck her head so hard I was alarmed, "inside here, and I pray every day for it to be filled up."

"You *pray?*"

"Certainly I pray." She was indignant. "don't you?"

I turned and went on. In our house only Mathilde prayed and it didn't look to me as though it did her much good, judging by her reception of Cecilia.

The fur flew the instant they set eyes on each other. I thought at first that it had to do with the great difference between them, Mathilde so ancient (she was my father's nursemaid before she was mine) and French-Canadian and fierce. But later on I wondered.

"You will clean your own room, Miss," Mathilde told her, lofty as a duchess.

"I wouldn't think of anything else," Cecilia said, so mild and serene, outranking her. "I can't stand having anyone messing around with my things."

Mathilde turned and sailed out of the room, with mutterings in her throat and her eternal beads swinging to right and left from her waist.

"Why did you have to be like that with Cecilia?" I said when she came to kiss me good-night.

Her black eyes as she bent over me were tender and bright. I had always thought her loving, and was disappointed to find she was only loving of me.

She sat up straight on the edge of my bed. "I told her a practical thing. We haven't got a staff of servants here!"

"You'd think we had," I said, "the way you run around waiting on me." The shrivelled hole in her face that once was a mouth pulled tighter, and I thought it was going to disappear. "You talk to her as though she were a Dickens orphan."

I looked at her critically, all bones, draped in black, with her dry yellowish hair standing up around her head in the way that made her look always surprised, though really she was surprised at nothing. Until now, when I opposed her. I had always been docile, her lamb, her little pumpkin: it made me sick, but I endured. Only I wasn't going to endure this: it was ungracious.

"Already she is making trouble here," she said snappishly.

"But that's unfair!" This was like early Roman justice. "First you insult her, then . . . "

I was stopped by an alarming sight. Mathilde's lower lip was trembling, and tears were wobbling in her eyes. Tears! I didn't know she could produce them: I'd thought her dry as a peneplainian drought.

I looked away toward the window, which was glowing from a blend of many lights: the last of the day and the beginning of the moon and a bright spotlight from my bedside lamp. They all mixed together in my eyes, as Mathilde sat there very still, and in my nostrils was her own blended scent. She always smelled of onions and apples – or lemons, or some other fruit: not on her breath, stale, but a fresh aroma about her clothes, and her hands which were always preparing these things for us. I could hear her hands now, creeping toward her beads. In the kitchen, her hands were swift and sharp, almost dangerous looking. But when she put a finished dish on the table before us, her hands had a different look: gentle and calm.

"And you don't have to tuck me in anyway," I muttered. "I'm big enough to keep my covers on."

She rattled her beads and made a great noise with her breathing, then left. I put out my light and watched through my window the beginning of night.

The night had a particular darkness. Though the darkness was holding off, it would come and I couldn't avoid it. Not as I avoided the war. There was a war on, involving all the world, but I merely studied it, along with the Medievals. It was represented to me as being about the same distance away.

When I complained about this my mother would say, "We're lucky to not have bombs dropping around us, or anyone of military age in the family. Just be thankful."

I was thankful, and it was this that worried me.

"Why," Cecilia asked, "have you got a nurse and a doctor? Are you an invalid or something?"

"Doctor Holtzman," I said, "is a friend of the family. He just happens to have delivered me into the world."

"Why didn't he ever let go of you?"

I ignored her; you couldn't tell her anything.

It was early winter: we were in our high boots and catching tiny silver fishes in the rock pools. I had tried to tell her their Latin names, but: "I don't want to know their Latin names, I know what they are!" She had thrown away her net and was catching them in her hands, which looked frozen. The fish were very alive, though she was a match for them.

"Are you really going to be an actress?" I asked, more or less to get back at her. (In three months she had never mentioned her mother.)

She raised her face. Her toque had blown off, and her hair was flying every way and glistening with spray.

"No, don't be stupid."

Well, that's what I thought. All that pretending to be someone else, it wouldn't suit her.

"But you said once . . . "

"The earth was all savages once!" She sounded like one of them.

"All right," I said very softly, but the wind blew away my words. She kept flashing looks at me. She hated to be held to anything she had said.

I removed myself, to a large pool of my own. What she'd said about Doctor Holtzman was eating me. He was strictly a friend of the family, I was sure, and only showed up so large because my parents didn't have very many friends. We seemed set apart somehow, sufficient to ourselves, in our own little world, which was a vast world to me and had everything in it.

Our two great friends, the Professor and the Doctor, most perfectly fulfilled, my father said, the Idea of Friend. They were like the two opposite ends of the pole, and for that reason we didn't often have them together; it was too upsetting for the Professor though the Doctor found it fun. He had a wicked streak in him and was my favourite.

My father favoured the Professor, because the Doctor was no good at all in a conversation. His mind wouldn't stay on a leash; he left everybody behind. Now and then my father would rope him into a game of chess; and he'd enter into it with a bang, full of gay threats and noisy plans, and sit there dynamically over the board with his big strong face thrust forward. He had red hair, very thick, very curly, and he'd run his hands through it when he was excited till it looked like a forest fire blazing around him. His whole face expressed itself when he talked, and he had pale piercing blue eyes, the kindest I have ever seen. He was deeply tanned summer and winter from fishing, and often had a fish for us, slung into his bag, wrapped in newspaper and then big slabs of sterile gauze.

But the chess never lasted long.

"This game," he'd cry, outraged, "is too damn slow!" and he'd push the table away so that the battlefield was a ruin. "Let's have a little action!" It was the Idea of Combat that had appealed to him.

My father would sigh and they'd go down to the basement and play ping pong, or dash away outside for a walk along the shore or a climb up the headland. The Doctor would come loping back in, his square muscular body giving off sparks, and my father failing and gasping behind him.

But he had a deeply philosophical side, which balanced him and made him a whole personality. His ideas were usually expressed in a burst, and briefly, for he hated extraneous verbiage.

"Words, words, more people have perished of words than of germs. Everywhere you go you find somebody mortally afflicted with dysentery of the mouth." ("Tsk tsk" from Mathilde and a rattle of beads, though she doted on him.) "It all began with the phrase, 'in the beginning was the word.' Folks took it to mean the word was to multiply, but the word was simply GO! . . . for the *people* to multiply. And by God they did. That's why we say 'from the word Go.' When are the heavens going to sound forth with a STOP? Say, what do you think is the latest in birth control?"

He often worked around to this. Mathilde would flee, and my mother would bend over her sewing, and I'd get very busy reading a book. I don't know what I'd have done later if it hadn't been for those newsy talks of his – which of course is why he did it.

Cecilia down the beach gave a shriek, and I went racing back to see what had happened. A wave had swamped her boots, and she was standing there laughing. It had such a merry sound I burst out laughing too. She lifted one foot and waggled a dripping boot at me, and this struck us as so hilarious that pretty soon we were pushing each other into the pools and soaked from top to bottom.

My merriment wore off as we squelched our way home. In the old days I'd have sneaked in and changed my clothes; but Cecilia couldn't lie. Whenever we did anything we shouldn't, and I wanted to gloss it over, she'd forget what our story was and get all muddled up and come out with the truth. Then my parents would give me that sorrowful look of theirs.

I looked at her, trudging along, squinting at her fish in her jar, oblivious of the wind and the wet. I was already coughing. I said, "What'll we tell them?"

"Who cares?" she said. "Tell them I did it."

Well I might be a liar, but I wasn't that bad. I told them the truth. And sure enough, Doctor Holtzman came running.

"I don't need you," I told him in the doorway of my room. "I've only got a cold." I'd just had a row with Mathilde, who wanted to put me to bed though dinner was just over. There was a weak chest somewhere in the family and you'd think it had been written into the will.

Cecilia was watching the whole thing from a distance. Right now she was wandering along the hall pretending to be blindfolded. Doctor Holtzman winked at her and she giggled. He was the only person who didn't talk down to her, or up, as I did, and they were pals.

I tried to push him out. He had his foot in the door.

"Come on, Hedleigh, I want to see that boat of yours."

"It's nothing, just a stupid boat." I'd been making it out of plywood. I only worked on it when Cecilia and I weren't speaking. I hated it.

"Boats," he said, grinning at me through the crack in the door, "are not noted for their intelligence." He pushed the door open. "Neither are boys. What's the idea going swimming at this time of year?"

He had his tools in his hands and was applying them all over me. "Come on, let's see that tongue."

I thought I saw Cecilia at the edge of the door. I stuck out my tongue in her direction. Better still I went over to the door and slammed it.

"She makes me sick," I said.

"Well there, you've admitted you're sick, now stand still

while I hear your chest." He fooled around some more. "Just a formality," he said, as he saw me scowling. "You're pretty important around here, Hedleigh."

"Yeah, like a king or something," I said bitterly. "Why can't they leave me alone?"

"You mightn't like that," he said gently. "To be alone isn't fun." What did he know about it? He was married.

But I thought of Cecilia alone in the hall. To have both parents die! How could anyone bear it . . .

I stood still and let him finish his examination, and swallowed the stuff he gave me. As he was going he slipped a chocolate bar into my hand. "Don't tell anyone," he said.

He'd forgotten to look at my boat.

I waited till I heard him running down the stairs. Then I went along the hall, looking into the shadows for Cecilia. The halls of the house were all dark because of the windows having, as it were, dropped to the bottom storey.

I found her in an alcove, looking out one of the small round windows at the moon. It was blurry and deep orange, just showing in streaks through a dark cloud. It looked like an eerie sunrise over a world that had been destroyed.

"Would you like a piece of chocolate?" I whispered. "Holtzman gave it to me." She watched while I broke it into two halves. I gave her one. "You see, he's just a friend of the family."

We stood together, not speaking, and watched the weird moon and ate the chocolate. It tasted faintly of fish.

The Professor never brought me chocolate, but he gave me dried figs quite often. He kept a supply of them in his pocket, and my mother sometimes lightly said he must have eaten a few too many. His throat gave off a dry sound when he spoke, as though dust were being disturbed there. At one time I thought it sounded attractive, and used to try to imitate it when I was alone on the beach; but I only succeeded in gargling and frightening the gulls.

Our lessons were held at home on Saturday afternoons. The Professor would stay to dinner and afterwards he and my father would settle into the living room for their favourite evening. In summer they'd throw open the windows and "relish Amphitrite's sweet thalassic air." In wintertime they'd pile a few half trees into the fireplace and toast their toes. The Professor kept a pair of huge woollen slippers at our place, for the purpose. "Warm feet, cool brain." He said it every time he put them on, forgetting he'd ever uttered the words before. He could remember everything that ever happened, provided it happened long enough ago, but nothing that went on around him. His mind was like my father's eyes, the way he had to hold a book an armslength away before he could read it, when he couldn't find his special glasses, which was most of the time. I wondered occasionally if there were any sort of special lenses you could get for far-sightedness of the mind, and if I would need them one day.

There they lay, sprawled out in their armchairs, their bodies limp. My father, though he was slight, was well-proportioned; but the Professor looked like an El Greco: frail and extended and ethereal. His long face was pearl-coloured, and fretted with tiny intricate patterns like morning frost, or a newborn baby, which he greatly resembled because of the transparent grey down that softly fringed his head at the top and sides. He had about him always a smell of books; and whenever he spoke, the skin on his throat fluttered like tissue paper.

Perched on my low, round, leather footstool close to the fire, I would listen while ideas arranged themselves in bright and orderly formations in the air. There was never any argument or interruption: above all no speech-making.

27

They added to each other's thought, with a "here I might interject," and many a "quite!" and now and then "I agree wholeheartedly and would merely qualify by pointing out . . ."

When the thoughts weren't aimed at me, I could take them in. I let them drift past my vision like the smoke from the fire; my imagination went out to meet them, and helped shape them into structures which filled the room and awakened in me mysterious responses. Lulled by the courteous drone of voices, and half-doped by the fire which grew hotter and hotter as my father heaped on the logs, I was aware sometimes of a strange awakening someplace far away within me; and this vigilance seemed almost to increase with my outer drowsiness. Inwardly I saw, clear-eyed, the heroes which populated the temples of cloud and smoke around us in the room. I watched with reverence old kings about to die, who, according to custom, had their body laid into a ship; and the ship sent forth, with sails set and slow fire burning it, that once out to sea it might blaze up in flame, and worthily bury the old hero at once in the sky and in the ocean.

What valour! Price of admittance to the Hall of Odin. The Valkyrs' creed, the everlasting duty of being brave. A man shall and must be valiant; he must march forward and quit himself like a man. The completeness of his victory over Fear will determine how much of a man he is.

But men then had other Powers than their own to call upon . . . and other Powers to fear. The Norseman could invoke the Summer-heat, the Sun, friendly Gods dwelling above in Asgard, the Garden of Asen. The empire of this Universe was divided equally between these and another race: Jotuns, the dark, hostile Powers of Nature, huge, shaggy, demonic beings, whose home was Jotunheim, a distant, dark, chaotic land. And between these two bands of Gods there was no reconciliation; they dwelt in perennial feud.

It happened sometimes that my inner activity reached a sudden end. Whether it was the Jotuns, or my father and the Professor lapsing into Latin, or just the hour . . . I never knew. It was then that I might interrupt and voice an opinion (in English), always something useless, I was sure. But they would both stop and turn to me as though Socrates himself had given forth an utterance. I would feel foolish and painfully unworthy. (Could I set forth in a burning ship? With no fire extinguisher on board?)

That was always my signal to myself to go to bed.

But when the information came directly at me, I got out of its way. I couldn't have said whether I had always done this, or if it was only since Cecilia started asking questions.

On a day in March I sat with the Professor and couldn't get my attention off the fire. I'd been watching the tip of a piece of firewood, which stuck out from the rest and caught the cold air and was having trouble igniting. It started to catch, glowed, faded, glowed again, and faded to almost nothing. I said to myself that if it caught, I could sail forth in a burning ship, but if it went out I was absolutely yellow.

"Archives was in the ancient ever," the Professor said, or something like that.

The glow came up brighter. Then it went out. I thought so, I said to myself, I knew it.

The wind was crying around the corners of the house with a cowardly sound, and I felt hopeless. I had left the Professor in Babylon. He didn't care, he was happy there. They believed, he said, that people lived again, they were reborn in later times . . . That caught my ear. I could imagine him living way back there, railroaded into now, dragging his heels all the way.

The end of the log exploded into light.

"Look!" I shouted, leaping out of my father's chair.

"What . . . wha . . . ?"

"The log caught fire!" I fell on my knees before it, ready to blow if it faltered.

"That," he said in mild astonishment, "is the customary reaction of wood to a certain degree of heat . . . "

I stood up and faced him. "Professor," I said, "what is the actual value of knowing about the past?"

"The value?" he asked. He was peering around me at the fire, trying to see past his big slippers, which were on the footstool in front of his face.

"Yes sir. The use of it."

"The use! Why . . . knowledge of our past enables us to set the right course for the future."

"Is the world setting the right course for the future now?"

"Presumably we are setting the best one possible, Hedleigh. That is to say we must assume so, since we are thoroughly apprised of past error . . . "

I'd caught him in a syllogism, but felt no triumph. My log was burning . . . yet there was some question in my mind. Beside my flaming ship was a charred log with a red eye in it watching me: glowing and looking, watching and glowing. I tried looking it down, but another sprang up beside it.

"Are you listening, Hedleigh?"

"Yes sir."

Then another and another . . . and the fire was full of eyes, all with a question in them, and the substance of them was painful. By the time I caught up with the Professor he was in the hall, putting on his coat.

"I sense that your heart is not in this today, Hedleigh."

"No," I said.

"It's your age." He wound his long muffler round and round his neck; it went on endlessly, as though he were a giraffe.

Funny he could say that to me, it's your age, but I couldn't say it to him.

"Yes sir," I said politely, wondering how old he really was and how long he had to live. It would solve a lot in my life if he were extinct.

Just then my father came into the hall.

"Ah Gerald," the Professor said. "I was about to go for a stroll. Despite the sound of the wind . . . have you noticed? – it mourns as though it has great problems."

"Well," my father said, "if it's worrying about how to blow Woehill House into the sea, it can cheer up."

He'd been repairing the cellar that day and was depressed. The old stonework was being eaten away; and if you tried to take a whole section out of it at once, to replace it with new, you had a collapse to contend with. It had to be done a stone at a time; he found this out when he tried restoring the old coach house at the back, and only added to its ruin.

They set out together, and I went back to the living room and sat for a long time poking the fire around, mainly poking the eyes out of it.

"Man," I said to her, "is so small against the elements."

"Woman isn't," she said.

I glanced at her to see if she were joking. She didn't look like it. She was standing with her feet apart, her hands clasped behind her, gazing boldly up into the firmament. We were looking at the stars from the thin patch of forest nearest the house.

"I hardly think," I said, using my father's most moderate

tone, "you ought to put your sex in such a superior position."

"It's you," she said, "that is putting your sex in an inferior one."

You "is" putting, I thought with disgust. What grammar!

It was a spring night, warm, with a warm wind blowing. The tall trees creaked with low, hoarse sounds, as though they were speaking in human voices. The sky was enormous, spread with branches and the stars sprinkled among them. Some of the stars that I was seeing weren't even there any more. The sky was as if remembering them. And others I was looking straight at and not seeing, because their light was still on the way; and these were like something the sky contained within itself but was not conscious of yet. And where was I located in my own consciousness? How did I really know that I was standing here? Maybe I was somewhere else, looking forward at myself, or backward: myself revisited.

Cecilia was elucidating her remark: "What is an element compared to a person? Can a storm have a baby? It can only kill them. So can men. That's why you go around memorizing all those wars. You're proud of them!"

Her thinking, I thought, is rudimentary. She made me see what the Professor meant by connecting brains and feet. She was always going around in bare feet and I figured it was this that overheated her brain.

"A woman," I said, "cannot have a baby without a man."

I felt suddenly embarrassed and wondered if she knew. My father had explained all this most beautifully, though it sounded pretty remote, and I doubted I should ever bother about it. Yet at the same time it was something central to manhood, rather like sports which he had always wished I'd get interested in.

"A man," Cecilia answered, "can't feed a baby."

It made me think of that business when I was four or five and a girl who was visiting left her doll behind and I got attached to it. The doll was wonderful, it wet its diapers, and my mother showed me how to change them, because I was all thumbs. Then one day my father came into the room, where I was putting the doll to bed. There was something about him, some mystery, something heavy in the air around him. He squatted down and spoke to me in a soft voice, his mouth smiling. He'd brought me a present, he said, and he put a box of little red soldiers into my hand and tiptoed out. But I had wanted something to love. I sat there wondering how you love a string of soldiers who are all stiff and whose arms and legs don't bend, and who certainly don't wet their pants. And when I turned and reached for the doll it was gone.

Be a little soldier, they sometimes said . . . for a man must be valiant. And "the completeness of his victory over Fear will determine how much of a man he is."

I said to her: "A woman needs a man to look after her while she looks after a baby."

"She does not!" Cecilia's voice came sharp and quick. "A woman and a child can manage just fine!"

Her father, I thought I had heard, had gone off and left them. So it was necessary for a woman to be valiant also.

"Pull!" she would yell. Her favourite game, tug-of-war. "You're not pulling!"

Half the time I didn't want to pull, I wanted to sit and read a book. I could pull her over, I knew: I had the physical strength. Yet when I got mad and really tried, I couldn't. She would stagger for a second and then fall back against the rope with a groan. I'd have to concentrate then, but I'd hear her, like an animal I heard once in a trap and never forgot . . . squeals and yelps and long low cries that could

33

be despair or even a kind of rapture. And one time when we had called a truce and I went to her, I saw two flashes of colour on her palms.

"Your hands are bleeding!" I cried out.

"They're not!" She thrust them behind her back. Her eyes were very bright and her mouth was pinched, but it broke into a grin. "Your heart's bleeding," she taunted me, "that's what it is, because I beat you!" She turned and ran away, swinging her hands around in front of her.

"You didn't beat me!" I shouted after her. "It was a tie!"

She turned toward me, her arms stiff at her sides, her chin sticking out. "In something like that, if a girl ties with a boy *the girl won!*"

That was her idea of the equality of the sexes.

"The balance of the sexes," Doctor Holtzman remarked one evening, "is just about right in this house."

I thought he meant because we were two males and two females: it was in the period that my father now termed B.C. (before Cecilia). But I realized later he meant that my mother was very feminine, and my father he regarded as well settled in his masculinity. My mother deferred to him, out of genuine respect, for she admired him. I thought it a natural thing that a woman should admire a man, and that the man should show concern and care for her, and lead her wisely, at the same time following where she led, when her heart led. He was the head of the family and she was the heart.

"It has to be, sometimes," the Doctor said, on the same occasion, "that marriage works. Or where would be the model for the rest of us?"

My father began to wave his pipe, cutting a path in the air for his words to follow: "The model, yes, the Platonic image, the hermaphrodite. Man and woman, originally one, severed and then ideally reunited, equal and opposite halves of the same being. And when they discover each other . . . "

He went on. Impressed, I glanced at my mother. She wasn't listening. She was still bent over the mending she was doing, but her eyes were on the Doctor, and her whole expression was one of sympathy. He was unhappily married, I had heard. He never talked about it but had let slip a hint just then. Perhaps that was why he liked visiting us, and why his big voice always softened when he spoke to my mother. For there was something about her that evoked the Idea of Woman in all of us. She was graceful and gentle and "walked in beauty," my father said. Everywhere you looked in the house you saw something she had embroidered or trimmed or stuffed; she made things with sea shells and painted figures and scenes on jars and glasses and plates. She never looked happier than when her face was smudged with paint or her fingers all earth from gardening. But they'd be clean and white again by evening for playing the piano, which she did beautifully, for she was musical through and through. Bird songs would strike her suddenly, and she would stop what she was doing and lift her head a little, listening. And then we would listen and hear what she was hearing and what had been there all along.

This was the same sensibility that you found in women like Mathilde Wesendonck, who inspired Wagner, and all the other women who lighted the way for the great.

"Women," I said kindly to Cecilia, "excel as inspirers. But they can't be great artists."

"That's what you think," said she. "*Women* . . . " her tone was fierce, "have been *waiting!*"

I decided she was definitely unladylike.

We walked back to the house in the bright night, over the ground all patterned with treetops. The wind had grown colder. The sea just below us was slurping as though drinking the land. And I tried to work out the Idea behind Cecilia. She was like sand in the spinach.

Whenever I was mad at her after that I called her Sandy. She didn't know why, and it made her furious.

But if my mother and father fulfilled, as I thought, the Parental Ideal, what was wrong? Wouldn't the Ideal be broad and inclusive? "We're a close family," my mother often said. And it seemed to me we got closer after Cecilia came; we closed in, we didn't open out to make room for her.

Frequently, when we were sitting in the living room, I'd catch a glimpse of her face in the doorway. My mother might be sitting on the arm of my father's chair, stroking his hair as though he were a kitten. He had fine, rich brown hair that fell back from his high forehead and nicely capped his head, which was well shaped; and as she stroked, he would smile up at her, his eyes making multitudes of creases at the corners. Or he might catch her hand and place it for a moment to his lips.

Cecilia might look in as she paused in passing but went on, while conversation altered but did not include "Come in."

Sometimes I went after her.

"What are you doing?" I might ask, finding her at the end of the hall, hesitating.

"Don't bother me, I'm busy!"

Busy winding a piece of string.

"What are you going to do with it?"

"None of your business."

"I only asked a civil question."

"You asked a nosey question, go on, go back to where you're wanted."

I'd go, and later maybe find her playing some great

36

game with the string. I'd want to know how it went. Humbly I'd learn, and kindly she would teach me. And we would be close.

But closeness had its opposite inborn; continually they shifted, now one side showing, now another. We were close, we were separate, then close again and closer for the separation.

The same when the breakages occurred; I sometimes sensed a mysterious constructiveness going on. The china lady who'd been reading to her child on the mantelpiece for a hundred years – I felt she was glad to go.

Not so, my telescope. When it went I turned on her: "Now, dammit, I can't see the sky!"

"What's the matter with your eyes?"

"Eyes aren't made for – "

Then her finger pointing at me, and her voice imperious: "To the tower!"

When one of us said it, it had to be obeyed. That was the rule. Away we went in a scramble, dropping everything. . . .

"Where are you going, Hedleigh?"

It seemed there was always a voice calling me back. It only sent us forward faster. I had Cecilia by the hand.

"Excelsior!"

We parted for the tower steps and went up singly, pulling them up behind us. There we faced out to sea and spoke as one, one mind, senseless, starting at any point . . . certain of arrival.

"Stars, oh stars,

"We cannot see thee, stars of night!

"Nor stars of day, above us in the blue. . .

"Below us too!

"Down through the earth and spinning off forever –

"Skies above and skies below. . . . "

She stamped her foot. I stamped mine. We stamped on the sky.

"And we in the middle

"of two skies."

Belowstairs let the breakage be. We knew the Universe was whole.

So I saw it on the morning of a summer day. The sun lay in yellow streaks across my ceiling, glowing with a special light . . . Was it the Idea of Day, or just the idea of a freedom day, the first of the summer holidays? I leaped out of bed, naked, as I always slept in summer. The air washed over me; my skin tingled as though rejoicing. Around me, as I pulled on my swimming trunks, the bright patterned walls vibrated. The day called and shouted outside my window. I went and hung out the sill, leaning into the air, already hot from a particularly blazing sun.

The sky and water were a solid sheet of blue; there was a slight haze from the heat, which hid the horizon line and blended them into one. They were a full circle enclosing all that my eyes could see, the headland slanting off to my right, and on my left the spikey pines with the gardens at their feet. The flower beds led one into another, then narrowed to a border that went all around the house. Out of it grew the roses which scrambled up to my window. I reached out and touched one, as though it were an electric current connecting me with all the rest.

Like a spark that had leaped the circuit, was the bright circle of flowers on the terrace table directly below me, where my parents and Cecilia were already at breakfast. The tabletop of pale green glass seemed to float in the warm haze, resembling an oval pool with red roses springing up out of its centre. It was punctuated at one end by my father's head, brown and richly shining, and at the other by a circle of gold – the smooth bun in which my mother always arranged her hair. Between them, like a black ink blot, Cecilia bent over her plate. Her intensity was almost visible around her.

My mother was tossing crumbs to a peppering of sparrows on the flagstones. Something she said made my father laugh, and the birds rose like a puff of smoke to the nearest tree. It was one of a crowd of firs, fighting for space on the edge of the lawn, just before the grass started slipping down in its many slopes to the water. Then one of the birds flew out toward the water and disappeared against a yellow sailboat which was bobbing along, flashing with a silvery light as the sun caught something on its deck. A great day for sailing, I thought, and turned back into my room and got going.

Downstairs, outside, I found the flagstones hot to my bare feet, and danced across them like a fakir (or faker as my father called them) on glowing coals. I headed for my mother, and kissed her. She was wearing a white dress with a bunch of violets at the neck; and her eyes seemed to belong to the flowing circuit of the water and the sky. She gave me a pat on the behind as I went past her.

"Why don't you kiss *me* good-morning and good-night?" Cecilia asked, and giggled.

"Because it would be boring!" I slid into my chair across from her.

I felt a silence and glanced up. My mother and father were looking at each other, my father smiling, my mother not.

Cecilia had her elbows on the table and was waving her grapefruit spoon slowly back and forth across her face, very evenly, like a metronome. Beyond the flashing silver, her skin was gold, tanned from a year of wind and snow

39

and sun. She was smiling behind the spoon, her wide bright smile, intimate today and taunting.

"Cecilia, eat your grapefruit!" my mother said, in the sharp voice she had developed just that year.

Spoonfuls of pure sunlight continued to pull my eyes from side to side.

"Who wants to go sailing to-day?" My father's voice was from a long way off, but still within the circle; for I felt as though I were swinging on the end of a rope, from one edge of blue to the other . . . and back . . . and to . . . and . . . I heard footsteps coming from the house, Mathilde, her shuffle, the dry clack of her beads, and then she stopped while still I swung.

"Cecilia! Uncle Gerald asked you a question! *Hedleigh!*" My mother's voice was frantic. The world swung past me, gaining speed.

There was a silent explosive movement: my mother's white dress obliterated the sun: then stillness. She was standing above Cecilia's chair; she had snatched the spoon out of her hand.

Cecilia looked up at her. I had thought of her as a little girl, but suddenly I saw two women staring at each other. I was aware of Mathilde behind me, very still.

My father's laugh broke the mood. "There was something," he said, "that we used to call spooning." His voice was calming to my mother, who went back to her chair and said in a mild tone:

"I'm sorry, Cecilia. It simply got on my nerves."

It was the first I knew of my mother having nerves. Mathilde, of course, had nerves, but she was religious. She came forward now with the basket of muffins she had brought and passed them around, warm and steaming.

Left with her grapefruit and no spoon, Cecilia didn't ask for another, but picked the fruit up in her fingers and began tearing it apart. She went about this lazily, a faint smile on her lips; and her shaggy hair fell over her plate forming two straight black curtains which seemed to enclose the little ritual. This time everyone was spellbound. It was as though we were watching living flesh give way beneath her fingers. I glanced at my father and saw on his face a look of fascination, and something else, almost like fear. Mathilde stood beside Cecilia, holding the bread basket high in the air, like a blessing or a threat. I didn't dare look at my mother.

When Cecilia raised the mutilated grapefruit to her mouth and sank her white teeth into it, her eyes rested on mine, and I was glad of my father's voice, saying firmly: "Hedleigh! I'd like more cream for my coffee. Go on out to the kitchen and bring me some please."

I followed Mathilde, feeling that the day was somehow getting ruined. It was cool in the big kitchen; the tile was a relief to my feet. There was a large fish lying dead in the sink; Mathilde's cat sat licking his paws and pretending he didn't know.

Mathilde banged the basket down on the counter so hard that the last muffin bounced out onto the floor. The cat came forward and copped it.

"She is bad enough," she said, yanking open the fridge, "she could be French."

"Bad?" I asked. "What's bad about her?" This interested me. I was always hearing about the good, the beautiful and the true; but information on the opposite was lacking.

"You never mind, you." Mathilde put down the cream and tugged up her thick black stockings, as though they were a charm to ward off evil. "All too soon you will find out."

She poured me some cream and I went back out, pondering the Idea of Mathilde. She ought to know what she's talking about, I thought, she's like a witch. She cooked with strange herbs that she found by the edge of the sea or in the forest. Often we'd see her prowling along, bent over the earth, trying to see what it might be hiding under a leaf or down a hole. In her black dress, with her basket over her bony arm, her hair a wild heap of straw, and her cat creeping by her side, she'd have gone to the stake in a minute in earlier times.

I sat down at the table and said, "I'm going fishing today," ignoring my father's earlier invitation to sail.

"*I*..." spoke Cecilia between clenched teeth, tearing out the last of the grapefruit, "am going *exploring*."

"Where?" I asked.

"Ah!" She leaned across the table, and her voice and her eyes were full of mystery.

"I'll come with you," I said. The day was shaping up again. I lit into a muffin.

"You said you were going fishing, Hedleigh." This from my mother, sounding irked. "Why don't you keep to your intention?"

I turned to her, surprised. "Because I've changed my mind."

"There is a difference," she said, "between altering a decision, in a considered way, and simply having no mind of your own." I noticed for the first time that her face was not fresh and smooth like Cecilia's. There were tiny wrinkles leading away from her mouth and up under her eyes, which were squinting at me slightly. And her voice was getting shrill. "It's a sign of weakness to be easily influenced by others."

"We're all influenced by other people's minds," I said, leaning back in my chair and gazing at the sky the way my father did in a debate. "It's one of the privileges of democracy. Besides – "

My father cut me off. "I see no reason to challenge a simple statement so elaborately!"

I stared at him in amazement. It was the kind of blind objection you'd expect to find in other homes.

"All right." If they were going to be primitive, I could too. "I'll go fishing if it'll make you happy."

"Now Hedleigh! I didn't say – " I didn't listen to what my mother didn't say.

A sudden wind had blown up from the ocean. It flung Cecilia's hair to one side, and she looked lop-sided, like the scraggly pines with their sea half all eaten away. Two lines of a poem, "On Weather-Beaten Pines," came into my head:

Is it with us as clearly shown
Which way the wind hath blown?

"It isn't that I *want* you to go fishing," my mother was saying. "You are missing the point."

Her voice had that overemphasis that people get when the Otherness in them is speaking. She was like a horn that somebody else was blowing. Yet the Other was herself too, deep and murky and foreign to her . . . and to me. I had once thought her simple and good; now I saw that she was complex and no one is good. At the same time, from another angle, her complexity was simple, in the way that all the great natural patterns are simple. She was sitting with her back to the sun; and as I gazed into the sun, she looked no more than a cut-out, lavender-grey, without features of her own, propped up against the pink roses on the hedge behind her.

"The point is that it's a bad habit to get into, letting your will bend unthinkingly, according to someone else's whim."

I was aware that Someone Else was listening from across the table. I glanced her way; she was buttering a muffin with slow loving strokes.

I said to my mother, "*You* change your mind sixty times a day to suit Dad."

"I'm a woman!" she said. "A woman is naturally more flexible!"

"That's plain rubbish!" I cried out, leaping to my feet.

"Hedleigh!" My father rose. "Kindly apologize to your mother!"

"Don't you dare!" My head swung between them. "We are not going to dignify a petty argument by – "

"If any person should apologize – " Mathilde was back, butting in as usual.

"Never mind, Mathilde, *please!*" My father sounded desperate!

She ignored him and said piously: "If ever a blessing would be said at this table . . . "

"Oh Mathilde, *not now!*" My mother stood in complete exasperation.

We were all standing except Cecilia, who continued eating her muffin with great calm. We watched her dumbly as she popped the last of it into her mouth and washed it down daintily with milk.

"Actually . . . " Cecilia rose to her feet, her voice reasonable and cool. "I prefer to go exploring alone, anyhow." She touched the corners of her mouth with her napkin and sailed off across the terrace, a skinny nutbrown Bernhardt in convict-striped shorts and jersey.

My father's laughter rose like a sea swell behind her and may have dimmed her triumph. I took off too, humiliated and furious, stamping away in the other direction; I rounded the hedge and threw myself on the grassy slope below the terrace. From there I could hear snatches of my mother's outburst:

" . . . used to be such a close family . . . discord . . . the type who – look how she smashes everything . . . "

There were gaps filled with the rush of water or comments from the seagulls or my father's "now now, Nora," his antidote for every fluctuation in the weather.

"... deeply affecting him, and in adolescence when every influence ... under a spell, there are some people ... her mother, quite unbalanced ... we should never have consented ..."

She didn't want her cousin's child, that was plain. There were times when I didn't want Cecilia either. But when I tried to remember what my life was like before she came, I couldn't get any real picture, just a mist with myself in the centre of it, perfectly still, like a ship becalmed.

I found her, late in the afternoon, at the entrance to the caves. She was crouching on the wet sand, her hair wild and stringy, and she looked like a sorceress, with the black holes of the caves in loops and humps behind her. She was making a word with broken seashells. She kicked the word to pieces as I approached her.

"Did you go exploring?" I threw myself down beside her, trying to sound casual, as though I hadn't spent the whole day looking for her. She would despise me if she knew that. Sometimes I felt she despised me anyway. It was hard to know what she thought; she was so separate and alone. I wanted to be like her and knew I never could ... and that if I could I would despise myself, the me I was, as much as she did.

"I sure did go exploring," she said darkly.

"Where did you go?" I asked, squinting at a low gull.

She flipped onto her knees, bending over me. "A simply marvellous place! Absolutely undiscovered until today!"

I stared into her eyes, with their black, burning, Clytemnestra look. Water dripped from her hair onto my face, her black hair that I envied, so definite a shade beside my own dirty blond. "Talk about spooky! You'd have been scared stiff!"

"You didn't go into the caves!" I pushed her back by her shoulders and sat up.

The caves were forbidden. Occasionally, with my father leading, and my mother and Mathilde standing in terror on the outer sand, we had ventured in with lanterns to investigate the outer regions. The inner ones had never been seen by human eyes. No one knew how many years ago they had begun to form. At some point the trees, which clung for their life to the thin soil on that mighty rock, started to sink their roots into the stone. Gradually they opened up a space for strands of seaweed to ease in and clutch them; and these entwined and matted, battering the honeycombs of rock at every tide.

The mass spread slowly and relentlessly, giving no outward sign. I often pictured it down there, spreading like a cancer, gathering weight and power in the darkness. I thought of it when the Professor spoke once about the principle of revolution; it employs, he said, an unknown alchemy of evil, by which constructive elements are combined in a particular degree and place to produce a force of pure, unalloyed destruction.

Cecilia had risen slowly to her feet and was smiling down at me with that look on her face that always upset my mother without a word being spoken. It was a look of knowing; but not as though she knew what she knew. It was more as if some Knowledge were looming behind her, terrifying and grand, using her eyes to look through, colouring them with that special deep dark blue. At such times she seemed not to see small obstacles like people.

"Now listen!" I said, jumping up.

"Walk around me once for luck!" She scampered away from me and swung around to face the North.

"Never mind the luck! *Did* you go into the caves?"

"Race you to the Nest!" she shouted, and we took off in a flying rain of sand.

She hadn't the Indian in her that I had, and her ankles and wrists were frail. I was taller, and wiry, and had grown up on the beach, while only a year ago she had thrown away her shoes. But the racing spirit comes from the heart. Pounding along the beach I was aware of the thrust of her jaw, and the impossibility of my winning. She would keep with me all down the sands and up the steep slope of the headland; and in the final second she'd tear a groan out of herself and lurch ahead.

We were there. Cecilia was dying beside me, flat on her face, gasping and strangling, her brown toes dug into the earth. I was laughing, but angry.

"Why do you do it?" I gasped. "You don't *have* to beat me!"

"Oh yes I do . . . oh yes, yes – *yes I have to!*" She rolled over onto her back, groaning and hugging her chest in agony. Tears were oozing out of her screwed-up eyes. Her smile was blissful.

"Well you're going to kill yourself one day!"

She went almost silent, and her eyes opened wide and fastened themselves on me. Suicide! . . . was she thinking I meant that? I said quickly, "You'll strain your heart or something. Next time I'll just slow down and *let* you win."

She thrust her face, dirt-streaked and threatening, close to mine.

"If you do . . . ! If you ever do a thing like that, I'll . . ."

"You'll what?"

"I'll . . . not love you when I grow up."

I almost smiled. A peace came down out of the sky and sat on me lightly.

"How do you know you'll love me anyway?"

"I don't."

"Then why did you say . . . "

"Oh shut up!" She swung away from me, rolling over a couple of times.

The Eastern sky was gathering for a spectacle of some sort, such as we often had after a brilliant day. I noticed now that the day had stayed brilliant right through, though it seemed to dim for a while. There was a pink and a blue rising up like a mist from the water, and meeting in a deep mauve high above; or maybe it was originating there, in the mauve sky, and separating out into the blue and the pink as it descended. It was hard to tell which way things were moving.

"The ocean," said Cecilia, a little distance away, her voice muffled, "knows."

"Knows what?" I asked cautiously. I didn't want my head bitten off.

"Certain things." She edged closer to me, travelling on her rear. "Like – it has to come in and out twice a day."

The ocean has no intelligence, I was going to say, but didn't. After all, it was deeper than men knew. Perhaps men too were deeper than men have known. Even I. Shallow around the edges, but then again in the centre . . .

"Yes," I said. "The ocean might even be compared with a person."

"Some people." She was beside me, watching me, while I watched the dark purple cloud gathering weight above our heads. "Some people are like the ocean, like me, I am."

"Yes," I said, "I know." I did know just then, though I hadn't before: in a way I hadn't known anything.

"And some are like the air." The air was warm, with something in it, a touch of cool like the scent of snow. There was a promise somewhere around. "And others like fire." And the sun sank all fiery toward the horizon, melting the mist on the water, leaving it clear and bright with silver spread across it. All the colour had risen into the sky. There was a line now between the water and the sky, separating them, making each one distinct, although they touched. "The best of them though and the strongest is earth. Capricorn, sign of earth, that's what you are."

"Am I?" I didn't know what I was, but decidedly I was, and the name could as well be one thing as another.

To her mysterious language she added ritual. She turned onto her knees and scooped up a handful of the soft brown earth, scuffed from our feet. She took my right hand and held it, palm up, and poured the earth into it, slowly, as we both watched.

Then, still kneeling, she looked into my face. I saw that the tears were still in her eyes from the effort of the race. "The ocean batters the earth," she said, her voice low and strained. "It has to, you know, to make sure the earth will stand firm." The tears slid down her cheeks to her mouth, white and parched and curved like a flower. "Aunt Nora was right this morning. You should go your own way, and make me follow if I'm going to, or let me not, but not follow me."

I couldn't follow her then.

"The earth!" She said it impatiently. "The earth stands firm!"

"Not always," I objected. "What about the caves?"

"The caves . . . " Her face was shining, luminous from the tears and from a strange happiness that was suddenly in her and that I knew through feeling it in myself. "The caves are what the earth and the water have made together."

Sounds were in my ears, birds and the wind whispering, and a drone of bees, sounds rising and falling as the waves themselves, or my chest as I sat there breathing and being. I almost felt the earth might be breathing too. It was warm, and seemed to give with me when I moved. I saw beyond us to the water all clear and the sky gathering its brightness, and I could not say where I left off and all of it began.

I was full of contentment and stretched out on the ground with a sigh.

"Where did you explore this afternoon?" I asked.

She tapped her head, smiling down at me. "In here."

"What was it like?"

"Ah," she said. "That's my secret."

She lay down beside me and we watched what was happening. All the blue of the sky had been absorbed into the enormous purple cloudbank, blackish now, that stretched like a carnival tent directly above us. Behind it the sky was bright and white; and across the white sky floated pink clouds in procession, each one edged with a band of silver light. The light brightened and then dimmed as the clouds approached the dark mountain in the middle. One by one they disappeared and were absorbed in it.

Suddenly, out of this, a shower began. We jumped up and met a light, white rain, hailstones! They were tiny and round and cascaded onto the ground with a musical roar, springing up in pebbly fountains where they struck. They pattered onto our heads and bounced off our hands, which we held out, laughing.

"It's a sign, it's a sign!" Her voice was joyful.

"A sign of what?"

"A sign that we can dare!" She scooped up two handfuls and made a bowl of her hands and let them run through, a milky stream onto the ground. "If something happens in a season when it shouldn't happen, it's a sign!" She turned her face to me, her cheeks pink, stung by the hail, her mouth laughing, hail bouncing into it. Her dark eyes were beautiful. "So will you? Will you dare?"

I would. I knew I would. What I would dare I didn't know, but yes, yes, without a doubt I would dare.

Our shoes made a sucking sound, a sticking and squelching, and the sound echoed all around and was caught up by the trapped wind. The wind had followed us in for a way, and now couldn't get out. It fluttered against my face, feeble and panicky as it died.

My eyes squinted into the darkness, but didn't see it, only the rim of light wavering up and down from my lantern. Cecilia held a lantern too, in her other hand; her near hand was in mine, tight and tense. We walked in step. We had not spoken.

Finally, "How long have we been in here?" I asked her. It felt like forever.

"Be quiet, five minutes."

"Well let's have a look and get back out."

She didn't answer.

I was cold, chilled through. We were wearing ski pants and heavy sweaters, but it wasn't enough. Nothing would have been enough. The ice age still lingered here. This was virgin slime, the original muck. We were bringing in the first light that had ever been. It didn't behave like light, lighting the darkness; instead the darkness swallowed it. The air . . . there was no air, just a wet heaviness, pressing down. It smelled of rot, rotting rot.

This was what came of signs and portents. Her mother, I gathered, went in for these queer things. The queerness was beginning to get me; I felt invisible creatures around us, breathing rage. Their rage became part of me, and I hated Cecilia for making me do this. If my parents knew!

"We don't have to go very far, you know." I spoke in a hushed voice. "The caves will be the same all the way. Once we've seen what they're like . . . "

"You go back if you want!" Her voice was always, strong and clear. She had her hair twisted up in a knot and was frowning. Her mouth was pinched like Mathilde's. She looked old and fierce, and I considered carefully before asking, "Well how far did you think we ought to go?"

"I'm going the whole way."

"The – the whole way? What do you mean . . . ?"

"As far as the caves go."

"But Celie, listen, we don't know how far they go!"

"That's why we're exploring them, you dope. Will you come on or go back?"

"If I go back, what – what will you . . . "

"I'm going to the end."

That was that. I couldn't let her go alone.

"Okay hurry up!" I tried to make her go faster. But she kept to her own pace.

The walls passing by slowly were blackish-green, with bulges of all sorts. In some places they were bloated, in others they shrank back into black holes that might contain anything. They curved up and met above our heads, but here too there was no plan or order: twisted shapes sagged low, trailing wet strands across our foreheads, or then again rose up into high vaults, like steeples, bent and crippled.

This bloat on the walls looked to me like a sickness, a great illness infecting the earth. It didn't show from outside: no one knew the extent of it. They would only know when everything collapsed and fell into the sea, Woehill House and all.

Cecilia was still tense, I could feel it in her hand, but more and more I relaxed. I drifted along, pulled by her hand . . . and by something else which seemed to be moving me. It began to be pleasant. The dark opened before us and closed behind, cradling us.

But one part of my mind stayed alert . . . a stubborn streak in the contentment, refusing it. To one thing I had paid strict attention from the beginning. Our path through the caves had not had a turn-off. We were following a single string of connected caverns. Outside, there were a dozen or more cave openings ranged along the shore; we had never known whether they had inner connections or not. This one, anyway, hadn't; we would be able to find our way out.

My attention even to this was trying to fall away; I clutched and got it back, then lost it again. It was like trying to hang onto a thought when you're falling asleep. I was colder too, and numb. I didn't know what was moving my legs. Cecilia too seemed propelled by a force not her own. Her head was bent forward as though she were fighting a wind, though the atmosphere grew more still as we went on.

Steps, steps, more steps, her hand in mine, still, my lips moving. I was begging her to let us turn back, but my voice came from somewhere else and I hardly recognized it as mine. Her face was like stone.

To be out of myself like this . . . Whatever I was was slipping away . . . I would soon be nothing, a flicker.

In the flicker, in the last small flame, there was something . . . the completeness of his victory . . . will determine how much of a – something – he is. I reached for the thought. How much of a *man* . . . his victory over – *Fear!* The recognition of it released it. Panic blossomed in me, like a root spreading out from my central being.

This! It was this I had always feared! To be sucked down . . . taken from the light of day and extinguished. In this fear I was Everyone. I stood at the heart. Heart of Darkness? This was the Soul of Darkness . . . home of the Jotuns – the dark hostile powers. Myth flickered, shifted dimension, became reality. An adult apprehending took hold of me; I saw through a mind heavy with Knowledge. I knew it of old: a force of death, of backwardness, destruction, in opposition to life! . . . progress . . . and love. It was what men have always called evil.

I saw it clearly. The Idea of Evil . . . and the reality of the Idea. I looked right into its eyes. It looked into mine and

53

was more frightened at being recognized than I was at recognizing it. For I saw that its essential secret is to be secret, to be denied, and that way to be free. Free to invade a man, to pull him down . . . and pull him up, up too high, then tip him down . . . down by way of up . . . like a plane caught in an updraft and spun from there into a hopeless nosedive. I had been too high on the headland.

I tore my hand out of hers and grabbed her wrist and swung her around to face me.

"Cecilia, we're going back. If you won't come I'll drag you. You may think I haven't the strength, but I have!"

She turned back without a word, looking as determined as before. Now it was I who set the pace.

"Step on it!" I pulled her along by the arm. Something told me we had to rush. I was rushing past an awareness on the edge of my consciousness, but I couldn't wait for it. It was a notion that at the heart of darkness was light: at the centre of No, lay Yes. It was illogical.

And another thought was keeping me busy. The sand under our feet was slightly more mucky than it had been. I looked down and saw the oily sheen of water-streaks in the lantern light. The tide was starting in. But we had allowed lots of time!

I kept my voice calm. "Tide's coming in." We kept glancing down as we hurried along. It was only a swirl; graceful patterns at our feet.

"It'll take ages to come in," Cecilia said. "Unless . . . " We broke into a half run. We were both thinking of how, occasionally, usually before a storm, the tide would rush in at high speed, doubling its pace.

Our rubber bathing shoes began to stick. "Kick off your shoes," I said. She did, and we left them there, four little red boats, upturned, swirling away behind us. Our lanterns swung faster, making lumps of pale light which crisscrossed each other in an agitated way.

"Hedleigh . . . "

"Don't talk," I said, and she obeyed me.

The water was up to our ankles. I kept my eyes straight ahead, piercing the gloom, straining with a terrific force. And maybe that was why I saw what I hadn't seen on our way in.

I jerked Cecilia to a stop. We held our lanterns higher and we looked, staring; it couldn't be, but was: a fork in the path ahead of us. Earlier, we had passed it by, not knowing the tunnel was branching off behind us.

"Which one do we take?" Her voice sounded trusting.

"I – I don't know." I thought frantically and decided it was the left.

"I think it was that one!" She pointed right. We stared at them both, while the water rose an inch.

Then: "It doesn't make any difference!" I was shouting, in my relief. "They'll both lead out to the shore!" I pulled her to the left, and we bent forward through the rising water. We struggled on through endless time, then suddenly, without warning, in the way of earthquakes and other cataclysms, the sound of the gushing water multiplied into a roar. We burst into a large open space, fretted with cave openings. Through each of these openings the tide was rushing at us.

"Hedleigh! Hedleigh!" Her voice was high and quivering, taut, like metal. A wave swirled round her legs; she half lost her balance and dropped her lantern. With a cry, she reached for it. I dragged her back. She crouched against me, and we stared at the tunnel mouths, which were beyond counting. There was no way to guess the one we should take. We lunged together into the nearest, and fought our way on.

"Mother! Mother!"

Did she say it, or I? One of us first, then the other.

When the water was up to our knees, Cecilia began to

scream. My mind rode on the waves of sound, so sweet and piercing. I marvelled at how long she could keep it up without a breath. Her long, attenuated cries appeared to take no strength from her body: her legs kept pace with mine in our push against the water. All my energy I put into each step, and to keeping my grip on Cecilia. I would soon let my lantern go, but her hand never.

And then – it seemed almost a natural act of the sea – we were caught up in the golden light of another lamp, and our ears were filled with the strong sound of my father's voice. He waded toward us, shouting instructions, which we obeyed: I dropped my lantern, put Cecilia's left hand into his right and gave him my right hand while he placed the handle of his lantern between his teeth. He led us forward against the sea in a victory V, he forming the peak of it, and the waters parting before him. I felt myself borne on a surge of miraculous interference. Striding, as it seemed without effort, my father hip deep and we up to our chests, we swept through the gathering light and broke out into dusk and the magnificence of the sky.

The sky this evening was heavy with storm clouds about to break. They drifted and overlapped, giving here and there a glimpse of a high beyond, which was bright blue and clear. It would soon grow dark around the earth, but the darkness would be nothing to the sun, still shining; and brilliant though it was, it was only a spark in a vast cosmic fire that never went out.

I kept staring upward as my father dragged us through the shallow water to the sand, and up the first rise toward the house. Above us, on the slopes of the lawn, my mother and Mathilde were in a wild fit of sobbing. They stood with their arms held out and their heads bent toward us. The lawn rose behind them, green and dark, and then the house, unlit, a large shadow of many shapes. My mother's yellow dress was flying every way in the wind, and her hair had come undone and was flying free too, golden in the last light of day. Mathilde was in her black, with a white apron; and only her apron and her face showed against the black trees, whose branches melted into the low, darkening clouds.

We scrambled up the rising terraces of the lawn, as the two of them slipped and slithered down toward us, their sobs growing louder. The wind was pushing us furiously from behind. Suddenly Cecilia tore away from my father, and turned around and stood, rigid, facing the sea. I looked up at the women above us and I understood; there were two of them and two of us, and both of them had their arms held out toward me.

Thunder crackled over the water, and an unnatural light parted the air. My father ordered my mother and Mathilde into the house, and they turned and went, still sobbing. Then he jerked Cecilia around by the arm and stood facing us both, dripping water, his face unrecognizable in its rage.

"Now then!" he shouted, over the wind. "Whose idea was that?"

"It was mine!" I said quickly.

Cecilia turned on me.

"You little liar!" she hissed. She swung to confront my father, throwing back her hair, hurling foam into my face. "I made him do it! He's trying to act manly! If he'd been manly he wouldn't have let me . . . "

"*Shut your mouth!*" my father bellowed at her.

As though sharing my shock, the sky opened up and the storm crashed over us. We stood for a moment, stunned, then I said through the deluge, "Hadn't we better go in?"

"Yes go in." My father sounded suddenly discouraged. "Get changed and wait in your rooms."

I took Cecilia's hand, but she yanked it away and ran on ahead of me toward the house.

I glanced back once and saw my father with the sea behind him. He stood like a statue, featureless and grim, his hair blown forward like a halo or a helmet around his head. As I looked there was a flash of lightning, and he seemed to rise up in flame, like a Viking king, consuming the dark of the sea and sky, taking all mysteries into himself and giving them forth to me in light.

Later I stood watching the storm from my bedroom window. The rain struck the window like splinters of glass, and the wind was trying to tear the ocean to pieces.

From time to time the whole landscape flared into view, every detail standing out in a pure white light. I could discern the stones on the headland, the leaves of the trees, the shoreline, and even blades of grass. And it was like that too inside my head, perfectly clear and sharp.

Cecilia had tested me, and I had almost failed the test. (Why had she wanted to? That was the thing I couldn't see. It was a part of the landscape that lay around the corner.) She'd been willing to give up her life so that my strength might be tested. Had she believed in it that much?

She was the child of an actress who had gone by choice to her death; and she had been ready to play out her role to its conclusion . . . but that I struck solid earth within myself in time. This point of strength was her gift to me.

And what of the timing? If I hadn't chosen that moment to turn back . . . and if my father hadn't come out onto the lawn, in the lull before the storm, to put away the chairs, he wouldn't have heard Cecilia screaming in the caves.

What about it all? The blackness lit up again . . . but here was my father's knock on the door.

I let him in. I could see that he had calmed down. We went to the window and looked out at the storm for a while, but he was not seeing the things I was.

"You know, Hedleigh," he said, sitting down on a chair beside my bed, "it's a natural thing at your age to want to rebel."

"I wasn't rebelling," I said. "I just wanted to see the caves."

"Yes I know. Well that's a rebellion, to go forward into mortal danger."

Or to go forward against the established order.

"The French Revolution . . . " I said.

"Never mind the French Revolution!" His composure cracked wide open. "I'm talking about here and now! You nearly lost your life today!"

Plenty of people lost their lives then, I thought. Fathers' and mothers' sons. They don't matter now. What will I matter in a couple of centuries?

He went on talking. Respectfully I kept my eyes on his face. But I had seen something larger than his face. "There is a reason, Hedleigh, for regulations and restrictions, for the rulings of older and wiser minds."

The older and wiser minds that got the world into this war. And all who are dying in this war . . . a hundred years from now they won't matter either.

Phrases followed: "concern for us" . . . "your mother's devotion" . . . "our life's hopes and expectations" . . . "your bright future. . . . "

Yet, strangely enough, small things mattered, very small things – the grass below as it had shown in the lightning . . . each blade of it, in a way, mattered. And my father's fear mattered greatly. There was fear in him: that was the Idea of his talk. I understood this and gave him the answers he wanted, and when he left he felt much better.

Soon after my father left, my mother came along the hall, on her way from Cecilia's bedroom. I braced myself and went to the door. I was ready for anything, but she simply put her arms around me and held me close for a long time without a word. When she left, I found my face drenched with her tears.

Much later when the house was silent, I went down the long hall to the isolated corner where Cecilia had her room. I found her sitting upright in the middle of her bed, with my mother's white cashmere shawl around her shoulders. There was no sound from the night outside, which had cleared and fallen still.

Cecilia was sitting in a square of moonlight, staring in front of her the way I have seen blind people stare. But she wasn't looking blindly: she was seeing. She didn't move as I eased onto the bed beside her. We sat quietly and looked together at what she had been seeing. I couldn't have told it, but if I'd had to name it I might have said we were looking at Death . . . and we were looking at Life. These were a pair of things which had to be seen out of the corners of our eyes, until such time as they might come together into a whole and we could confront them. They were not accustomed to being confronted. They hid in the highest hills, or in the depths of everyday experience, and when people turned to look at them they vanished. They held the world in their two hands, and both were feared, in their different ways, and even disbelieved.

And my life . . . what would I do with my life, now that I had it? (I had had it before but hadn't realized it, and so had not really possessed it.) I knew that I would create something, that to create was the true and proper work of any human being, man or woman. To create with the hands or with the mind and imagination, or with the body as a woman does . . . it was all the same thing, in different ways, the same thing as the creation of the world and all the universes, however that had happened.

Cecilia stirred. I looked at her, and found her looking at me.

There was one thing we had never talked about.

"Did your mother really kill herself?" I asked.

"Yes," she said peacefully. "I'll probably do the same."

I took her arm. "You can't do that!"

"Why not?" Her eyes were shaded from me, the moonlight streaming on her hair. "My life belongs to me."

"It belongs to other people too!"

"What other people?"

"The people you belong to."

She was silent. Not the sea nor the air stirred. Her hand lay white and thin against the white shawl, and her lips too were white in the white moonlight. They barely moved as she said, "Who do I belong to?"

"Let's get up early tomorrow and go for a hike through the forest," was all I could say.

"Tomorrow?" she gave a giggle. "It's tomorrow now."

"It is not," I said, "it's last night."

We began to laugh, and couldn't stop. Soon we were howling, stuffing handkerchiefs into our mouths so that no one would hear. We rolled around on the bed, pounding each other with our fists, our knees and elbows tangled up in my mother's shawl. Once Cecilia's foot hit my eye, and that set us off at a higher pitch so we nearly strangled. My chest was full of pain, and at moments we sounded as though desperately weeping. Toward the end I saw her lying backwards, her head hanging over the edge of the bed, her fists pressed to her temples and her hair brushing the floor. She looked like Ophelia, drowning in merry tears.

At last we were worn out and lay together in a heap. I felt smooth and clean, as though my bones were polished. Cecilia's eyes gazed into mine, bright with peace and tears, behind her long lashes, slowly lowering.

I got up and helped her into bed. My mother's shawl was on the floor, soft under my feet, as I tucked her in.

"Maybe you belong to me," I said, and pulled the covers

up around her shoulders. She was asleep before I lifted my hands from them. But I had spent quite a while looking at her face.

The next day there was peace over the land, and over the water, with its lazy gulls again. And a supernatural peace hung over the terrace table, where I was having lunch with my parents. Cecilia had gone off alone on a picnic. We had walked in the morning and climbed a high hill and seen for miles around in the especially clear day. Mathilde was in bed with her nerves.

My parents were always relaxed when Cecilia was absent. But their manner today had an added relief. They chatted about small things of all kinds. Every small thing, I thought, is part of some larger thing. And the larger ones belong to a larger again. We see a division line between things, but later perhaps there is not.

And where had the storm gone that was? Or had it merely been imagined? All of us, perhaps, only imagined by some Mind . . . a pack of Ideas in disguise. The Mind tilts us this way and that. Have we any say in the matter?

"Or not, Hedleigh?"

"Not what?" My head snapped round toward my mother. They both laughed. She enunciated carefully, her voice tender and fond: "Do you want some strawberry shortcake or not?"

Her smile was bright as the bright sunlight. But a silver tooth flashed darkly in her mouth. It had always been there, marring her. The sun had spots on it too, if you cared to look.

"What if I don't want to teach History?"

I hadn't meant to say that. It popped out, like somebody hiding behind a door, suddenly pushed from behind.

There was a brief silence. Then my father asked, "What's that got to do with strawberry shortcake?"

My mother said, leaning forward, her eyes glinting strangely in the sun: "Who put that idea into your head?"

"Does an idea have to be put into my head?" I was furious because it had been.

"All right, Hedleigh," my father said, "if you don't want to teach History, you needn't."

Those shadows under his eyes, I realized, had been there for years. And the grim look about his mouth as soon as his smile ceased and the crinkles died down from the edges of his eyes . . . There was some lack of happiness in him.

I turned my eyes to my mother. Her mouth was tense, pulled in a little at each corner. A memory came to me of sharp words from her mouth, behind closed doors. No life was perfect.

"Hedleigh . . . " my father gaily speared a slice of bread, "is going to have to decide what else he would rather do, that's all."

"That'll be easy," I said.

We finished lunch in silence. I made a great point of watching the gulls. My mother was watching me, but I pretended not to notice. I glanced once at my father and he smiled quickly. I felt a strange power in me, a power to hurt. It thrilled me in a way and frightened me.

I felt it again, face to face with the Professor.

"What's this I hear?" His old features were trembling, his mouth pink and soft – not a manly mouth, I thought. "You do not want to pursue your career . . . ?"

My father was behind me in the living room, and must have gestured. The Professor's voice wavered. He looked beyond my shoulder and said, "But surely . . . a modicum of reason applied – " and stopped again, as a soft disturbance broke the air, such as a brush of birds' wings, or my father perhaps flapping his hands.

"Hedleigh will make his own choice of career." He came around me, touching the Professor's arm in a friendly way, holding him up I rather thought. "When the time comes. He's young yet."

But I was not so young, not as young as they thought. I felt equal to them; sorry for them too, with their beseeching looks. Too much of their happiness hung upon me, what I chose to do. I talked History with them then to cheer them up, and they thought I was giving in. They didn't know there was a difference between giving and giving in. There were certain things (I was starting to realize this) that looked alike and definitely were not – like begging and praying.

"Who," I had asked Cecilia once, "do you pray to?"

"Well who do you think I pray to?" she snapped back. "Do you think I pray to myself?"

It wouldn't have surprised me if she did. I was certain she didn't go down on her knees like Mathilde – who then tried to bring everyone onto their knees before her. Cecilia, at least, forced people to stand up.

But who could stand up to her? Not my parents. They got the Doctor in to talk to her. He came in quietly, as though there'd been a death in the family, passing me in the hall on his way to the living room, where Cecilia was waiting for him. He looked at me for a moment. I saw a deep sad look in his eyes. It wasn't there on my account; it was not that recent. It was a greater sorrow going back through his life and long before. I saw him clearly, carrying everywhere in his hand a small black bag and in his eyes the Idea of Suffering. Was it the second, more than the first, that made him a healer?

He went in to Cecilia and I had no way of knowing what transpired between them. I passed by the living room a couple of times in the hopes of overhearing. They had left the door open but were speaking in soft voices, bending over a little book on Cecilia's lap.

Cecilia had a secret book. I had a secret book too, my diary, but there was nothing in it worth reading, only events. I left it lying around everywhere. Not she. Her small black book with gold lettering on the cover rode around with her in her pocket and at night went under her pillow, so she said.

Men, it was joked around at school, were supposed to have a little black book, but not women. (What was all this about men and women and their supposedness? A man is this, that and the other, a woman is something else again.)

A woman is certainly secretive, anyway. "It's my *secret!*" she would say, with accusation, when I surprised her reading it, and she'd hold it behind her back, staring me down, until I left her. Now undoubtedly it was this book she was discussing with the Doctor. It gave me a horrible feeling, which I realized with surprise must be jealousy.

When he had gone, I accosted her. "I thought that book was a secret."

"It's *my* secret," she said, high and mighty, "and I can share my secret with whoever I like."

*Whom*ever I like, I thought to myself. She would never learn English, I'd reconciled myself to that. It was the one bit of ground on which I could feel superior to her, so I probably didn't even want her to.

My superiority. This, a man was supposed to have – or kid himself he had? There was manly and manly, and one was the real thing, but the other was more inclined to look like it.

And there was separate and separate. I felt most separate when surrounded by my parents, my nurse, my teacher and my doctor. And when I would see Cecilia, alone and apart, far down the beach or high up in a tree beyond the reach of voices, I felt she was in some marvellous company, which I envied.

And who, anyway, did one pray to, if not oneself?

My father often found it necessary to pray to Mathilde. She had not spoken to Cecilia since the caves. She served her at the table looking past her; if Cecilia spoke she was deaf. I heard my father trying to reason with her. They were in the kitchen at night, while I skulked around the dining room door.

"Mathilde, I wish you would try to be charitable! Doesn't your catechism tell you . . . "

"My catechism" slam of a drawer "says *thou shalt not kill!*"

"She didn't kill him!"

"That was not her fault! She has the devil in her, that one!"

"That may not be her fault either."

"It is anybody's fault that lets the devil in! He comes around knocking everywhere, and we can bolt up the door or throw open it wide!" She always tangled up her English when she was mad.

"I think your devil is smarter than that!" He blamed the devil on Mathilde. "I believe he devotes more of his time creeping in the back door of holy houses . . . wearing the disguise of an angel. There he causes sulks and tantrums."

"Who . . . " bucket across the flagstones "is having a tantrum? That was you all your life when you were little!"

"Mathilde, for pity's sake, I was not little all my life!"

And she, furious now: "You maybe don't think so!"

"The topic of our talk is Cecilia! Now I want you to act as though nothing had happened!"

"Act? ACT?" The cat came whizzing out of the kitchen, streaking between my feet. "There is enough acting around this place here! It needs for somebody to be honest! Next time it may not turn out so harmless!"

"There won't be a next time," my father said. He sounded very sure.

He came into the dining room and saw me there. I hadn't moved.

"Have you been listening?" he asked.

"Yes." Why bother lying?

"It's a difficult situation," he said, seriously.

We strolled out onto the lawn to look at the night. "The whole business of getting together," I remarked, "is the trickiest business there is."

"I think, Hedleigh, you have put your finger on the heart of things."

This would have pleased me before. But why bother with conceit?

And why bother, either, to fight? Or to care a great deal? They told me the next day in my room, my father in his most Reasonable Tone, my mother standing by in case of need. It was perfectly logical and couldn't be challenged. Cecilia was being robbed of educational advantages here. She had shown a flair for art, and there was no one to teach her. As she eschewed the local school and was *non sympatico* with the academic subjects offered by my father and the Professor, she was receiving no preparation for life. It was not fair to her. And then, she'd been raised in a city, an American city, and all in all that is where she would be happiest.

This appeared to be the end of his soliloquy. I said,

"Okay." They seemed to expect me to say something more.

It didn't lend itself to comment. I wrote in my diary: Cecilia leaving.

She was being sent to my mother's sister in Baltimore, my Aunt Sheina whom I'd never seen, and her husband Frederick. Uncle Frederick was an artist, and difficult, so it was said, though they never said how he was difficult. It was related to the reason that my aunt never visited us. She didn't feel she could leave him. I thought possibly he was a cripple.

Their children were grown, and they had space for Cecilia in the house. She takes up a different kind of space, I thought. But I was keeping my thoughts to myself. And even I was not really on the receiving end of them.

In the tower. And she was going the next day. Going. It was all we could think about.

"Going . . . " one of us said.

"Going from here

"to where?

"where is there

"there is only here

"here and now!

"Send me a letter.

"What letter?

"*u!*

"Or why not *i?*

"Same thing.

"And we will meet

"in time

"or out of it

"in no time!

"Then we'll be
"here!
"where I
"and I
"I am
"and we
"we am!"
(Our laughter.)

And I heard her laughter often the next day as she dashed around, preparing, packing . . . already gone. Movement suited her. I sat in my room and watched the grey day through the window. The day and the clouds passed slowly, as though leading to others; but I could not foresee them. Only the evening lay ahead, heavy, like a hardness in my chest.

"Good-bye!" She leaned out the car window. "Bye! Bye bye!" She looked excited and happy, waving a green scarf. A silver bracelet was shining on her wrist – a Christmas present from my mother. Next Christmas they wouldn't have to go through the pretence.

I stood alone in the driveway, waving. My mother and Mathilde did not join me; their smiles had run out early in the day.

Cecilia pulled her head in and started chattering to my father at the wheel. I caught a flash of her face, bright and animated, as they drove off. She didn't look back.

A separation stretched between us: a distance which might extend forever. At one end she, going forward: at the other I, left behind.

Then it was that it struck me. It hit me like a ton of bricks. I was alone on the earth, alone and unfriended, just as alone as Cecilia. I went back into the house and saw my mother standing there, and I walked past her without a word.

Year Two

Going and returning: I see the one within the other. She drives away calling good-bye, and at the same time walks out onto the terrace two years, as it seemed then, later.

"Hello."

I said, "Hello." And that seemed to be the whole story.

An episode, like an evolution or a life, is simple in its beginning and at its ending. The complexities are in the middle part. I looked back, as I look back later, now, and saw – as I see – the complex made simple. It was as though she went down with the sun and came back with the morning; the dark night was over, sunk into the perpetual Sun which casts a shadow only where it meets an obstacle.

She left in the autumn, as she had come, and returned in the autumn to stay until another summer, tracing a circle around my life, delineating me, separating me from that which would absorb me if it could. She was familiar when she left me, and a stranger when I saw her again; yet viewing the familiar and the strange with a single eye, I see that the stranger was in her when she left, and someone as familiar as myself came back.

Our strangeness was on the surface only, like the make-up she wore on her face. Under the rouged lips was her smile; beneath its uncertainty her old Knowledge.

We stood there – how long? "Hello" . . . with the Idea

crowding into my mind. *Hello*, the Word Go, word of life; as Good-bye is the word of death. Two points pulling oppositely, yet meeting somewhere after all.

"You're taller," she said, looking from my head to where Molière lay on the flagstones. A second time she had walked into my life and found me reading, and brought me to my feet.

"And you're very chic." You have cut your hair. How could you? A little black cap, with waves put in. And tiny pearls in your ears. Did you think you were not enough?

"What have you been doing?"

"Nothing," I said. "Nothing much." Waiting, that's all. Holding my ground. I gained a little ground when you were here; I've managed to hold it. But I haven't known how to push back the frontier. Now that you're home . . .

"Are you home to stay?"

"Home?"

Just the tone. That's all I need (and the look in your eyes) to catch the whole Idea. Home, the primeval place, place of belonging; shelter from the outer darkness.

"I really wouldn't know." She laughed; but in the laugh was something else, far from laughter.

"I hear you've been painting." Taking lessons from Uncle Frederick, so they say. You didn't write. Aunt Sheina wrote, but her letters were strange. There were undercurrents, Mother said, though she didn't say it to me. Wherever you are there will be currents of many kinds. You are good, they say. Do they mean at painting?

"Is the Professor still alive?"

"Just." He has taught me everything he knows. It isn't much. It's none of the things you meant when you told me: "There are other things to know." Later I asked him: "Are there other things to be known, do you think – dimensions we don't even suspect?" But the Idea went into mist.

"Your voice is different."

Yours isn't: it's musical still, and clear. But you've changed in other ways. You were skinny; now you're slim. And taller . . . or is it the little heels on your shoes? I am shy, shy with you. Imagine! There was never that when we were children. There was a sameness about us then; we stood in the same place. Now we are separated by some great distance, and straining across it.

"Did you like Baltimore?"

"Like Baltimore?" Again that laugh, not a laugh. "A city is a place you live in. If you have to."

And you don't have to any more. Why did you leave so suddenly? Was it suddenly? My father has been renovating the coach house! He's had workmen in . . . making it self-contained. So that's what they're up to: they're putting you out there.

That meant they had known and hadn't told me she was coming back. I confronted my mother, where I found her in the living room, while my father showed Cecilia her quarters.

"We thought it would be a nice surprise for you, Hedleigh!" Her smile looked pasted on. "You've missed Cecilia, I know."

"Thanks for telling me." My voice hadn't meant to sound bitter. "Why isn't she living in the house?"

"She'll be joining us for dinners. She's a young lady now, you know, she needs room to herself."

A letter opener that she was tinkering with caught the sun and flashed in my eye. She sat very straight, in her blue dress, looking past me at the blue water, and her blue eyes were cold. "And she paints now, I understand she's quite immersed in it all. She needs a studio."

"She could have a studio out there and still live in the house!"

The letter opener hit the desk with a clatter, seeming to rip the smile off her mouth. "It's only a few steps to the coach house, my dear! When you want to go there."

Outside a woodpecker tapped a steady beat. I looked into my mother's eyes and saw my enemy.

"Okay, Mother. Thanks. I had overlooked that simple point." That's why they hadn't told me she was coming. They'd been hoping for a last-minute save. "What brought her back anyway?" I asked.

She stood and faced me, tilting her head up just a little as she had to now. "That . . . is not your affair."

I knew by the way she said it that it was.

I went out to the coach house. The door was wide open and I stepped inside and was dazzled by the newness. I had grown used to Woehill House, with its black beams, sagging and slanting, and its rippling floors and pockets of darkness. Everything here was in perfect alignment. The new woodwork delighted my eye with its strong clean lines; and the room was brilliant from fresh paint and from the sunlight flooding in, streaming down from the skylight and in through the enormous front window, which also caught the glare of the water; for the coach house was on a rise behind the main one and had a clear view. It was brighter in here than outside, as though the light had been captured and intensified. The place smelled of turpentine and new wood. There was a kitchenette in the corner, behind a half wall, and many long shelves and a lounge sofa with cushions in vivid shades.

I hadn't paid much attention to the rebuilding. They'd mumbled something about guest space. Now the guest was here, standing in the middle of the big room. She looked up at the sky through the roof, and around at the walls of golden pine.

She said, "It's my own, isn't it?"

"I guess so." I felt strangely jealous of it.

"It's nice."

"Very nice." I would have hated to be so far from everybody.

She looked small again in the high, wide room. She had kicked off the shoes with the little heels, and was stationed in her stocking feet at the exact centre of the large circular hand-hooked carpet. It was composed of whirls, one bright colour leading into another, and she looked like a bull's-eye standing there, a target for people to aim at. I remembered the first day when I had kissed her on the cheek. I would not dare do that now.

"Can I help you some way?" I asked her. "Unpack your stuff . . . " There was a big crate standing on the floor; it might be paintings. I was anxious to see them. Behind her on the window seat was a crowbar, probably brought in for the purpose.

"If you want."

No more now than ever was she full of glee at my presence. But as I drew near her to fetch the crowbar, her eyes fixed on me, deep and dark, and she said in a gentle way:

"I got all your letters."

"Oh did you?" I stopped. "I didn't know."

"I liked them."

"Well I'm glad."

"I didn't write because . . . "

"I know." I knew suddenly that a letter is second-hand, merely a telling, not experiencing, and foreign to her on that account. I was beginning to recognize her. The neat cap of hair was tumbled by the wind, and the pearls glowing on her ears looked a natural thing, as though still in the shell. Her lips were their own pale colour again; and there was sweetness in the smile.

I smiled too. "Good luck in here. Be another Gauguin – or whatever you want to be another of. The first of yourself, I guess. Be one for me."

She laughed, her own real laugh, and laid a finger lightly on my arm. Then she spoke the old words:

"Walk around me once for luck."

I trudged round her in a circle, laughing.

"But dare not walk around me twice!"

"Hey!" I stopped, and stopped laughing too. "Did you mean the rest of it?"

But if thou walkest round me thrice, I'll marry thee.

We looked at each other and a silence spread around us, like rings of water from a stone thrown deep. Each ring told a different story, though all were connected by the same impulse. As I looked down, the pattern on the carpet seemed the same, but in reverse. My feet were on the red outer ring, which blended into orange, then to yellow, and onward, inward, the colours meeting, joining, moving to the centre where she stood.

Her feet, in their stockings, moved. She came quietly to me with the crowbar, and I took it and attacked the crate, feeling a wild joy in the action.

"Wow!" I said, gasping. The thing was sealed up like a Pharaoh's tomb. "Did Uncle Frederick put this together?"

"What – him?" She gave a funny laugh, rather harsh.

I looked up. "What's he like?"

"Be careful of those paintings, mind you don't dig them," she said, and giggled. She began running around, strewing books along the shelves and shoving handfuls of clothes into the dresser. Tidiness, I thought, is still not her outstanding characteristic. I recalled Mathilde saying she would keep house like a sow.

"Why don't you stand those books up?" I asked her.

"Then you'll be able to see the titles."

"Titles aren't everything," she said blithely, snapping her fingers at me.

"They're pretty important for a book."

"I'll find what I want when I need it, don't you worry."

Anyway, I thought, how can you go around a person three times if you can't get round them twice? It's like the challenges in the fairy tales, which everyone knows are impossible.

I finally got the front panel pried away. At that point she hurried over.

"Here," she said briskly, "I'll see to those."

"Well can't I look at them?"

"No!" She laughed. "You're not a buyer."

"Are they only for buyers?" She was standing close to me, trying to push me away. The air was filled with fragrance, like roses steaming in the sun. I tossed the front panel to one side, and she clutched at it, dashing around behind me.

"Maybe I'll buy one," I said over my shoulder. "How much are they?"

"You couldn't afford it." I had hold of the first canvas, and was slanting it outward on its thin wooden edge. Her voice sharpened suddenly: I was amazed at how sharp it was. "Okay now, Hedleigh, get your hands off that!"

Her tone put a fear in me and I dropped it. It fell forward against my knees, and she curved round, bending over, to retrieve it. Behind it a large sheet of grey paper, unmounted, had sagged. I stared down into it, into the deep curve, and the picture that was on it in delicate pastels.

It was only a glimpse. With a gasp she swooped and snatched it up, holding it behind her back.

I had seen it, the young nude girl, with her soft shapes, pink tipped, and her limbs folded gracefully. The look on the face too I had seen, eager and a little frightened, but trusting.

The same face confronted me, pale and furious.

"Who do you think you are?" Her voice was low and shook slightly. "Barging in here and smashing things right and left!"

"That's all right, Cecilia." I spoke with great reasonableness. "I know perfectly well . . . any civilized person knows . . . that in art the human form has a – an aesthetic . . . " My voice was shaking too. "Anyway," I added, "your life's your own."

"Thank you *very much!*"

She stood there breathing fire, her eyes smouldering, blue as midnight and far more beautiful than in the picture. And was she all . . . ? My thoughts tumbled, wild and colliding.

"It's quite a good painting," I said. "Pastel, isn't it?" I wanted to see it again. I would like to have possessed it and stared at it all day, all night. "Who did it?"

"Frederick." The word was a dismissal.

"Do you mean Uncle Frederick?"

She gave a brief nod. "He wanted me to pose for him."

We stood there with only our breathing and our thoughts, mine all in a twist.

"When did you stop calling him Uncle?"

"Get out of here," she said calmly.

I stayed where I was. "How come you've got the picture?"

"He gave it to me."

"He wanted you to pose and he didn't even want the picture?"

In her look I saw the answer. He had wanted something else.

And was it something he got? I searched her face. Her gaze didn't waver, and relief started through me. Then she dropped her eyes, as two flaming circles appeared in her cheeks.

The wave that had started in me turned to rage. It swept me across the room and out, hurtling me down the slopes and along the beach. I was in a passion of loss . . . before ever I had known passion of love. There was fury in my feet as I kicked the sand, in my hands grabbing up stones and flinging them into the water, and in my arms, whirling, as though I were marooned somewhere and desperate, dying.

When I had done dying I threw myself flat on the sand, out where the tide had withdrawn, and stared into the darkness of my folded arms. It must come clear if I tore into it with my whole brain. Everything could be thought out: of this I had been assured. Reason could restore order out of chaos; man was master of his fate, of nature's elements and his own.

So that's how Uncle Frederick was difficult . . . that way, women, or girls – just girls perhaps, young and innocent as she was and never would be again. My unmanly tears I blamed on the wet sand pressing into my face.

Here we had run laughing in the waves, thinking the world as clean as ourselves in our childish bathing suits. But under our suits all the time we had worn the age-old badge of sin, our human bodies. From these . . . the body of mankind, and its most awful pains. Object of worship, for its beauty and possibilities of pleasure, its possibilities for agony also had been explored, and developed to fine crafts by fiends in torture chambers.

Good and Evil, another eternal and opposite pair, were inseparable, it seemed, from Man and Woman. They were in some way tangled. You never met one without the other close behind – or leading. They travelled full circle, all locked in together, as I was locked in my dark arms.

That night I had a dream. The Professor was teaching me, and I was listening. We were positioned somewhere in the highest sky, standing on nothing, lit by a million stars. Below us we saw the world, a perfect circle, intersected by two lines of force running North and South and East and West. (I had seen this before. Or was it that I would see it again? Perhaps I had always known it.)

The Professor didn't say much, yet it seemed he said everything, more than all the words he had ever spoken. It was simple and central, and everything else spread out from it, like the points of the stars and the light rays of all the years. He compared West and East with Man and Woman; North with Good and South with Evil.

"The two directions constitute two different lines of force," he told me. (He seemed more to be thinking it than saying it; yet I heard him.) "North and South are antagonistic opposites; East and West are complementary. Good and Evil pull in opposite directions, one desiring the advancement of the individual and the world, the other its destruction. They cannot be reconciled. Any attempt to do so results merely in compromise, never in completion. The ideal is to achieve a greater and greater separation between them, so that each may be recognized for what it is, and dealt with accordingly. The movement of the other pair, however, the sexual, is toward each other. There lies wholeness. The aim of everything is that they should come together and hold the other two apart. The others will meet too, but beyond the circle and beyond our comprehension."

It was already beyond mine. I looked at him and saw that he was not the Professor after all; it was only that he was a teacher . . . and not particularly he or she, but could have been some of both – a little like my mother and my father, I decided, on waking up.

It was dawn, and a dawn was breaking too inside my

head. It had nothing to do with the dream; I merely saw with vividness the inequality that existed between Cecilia's life and mine. Once again she had been expelled too soon from her childhood. Always for me the safety and the shelter, and for her the great and awful experiences that ought at least to wait upon her years.

From my bed I could see the top ridge of the sun just breaking the horizon. I got out and sat on the bed, cross-legged in the way of my ancestors, and watched for a long time, barely thinking, while the sun rose. At one point it came into position against the central crossbars of my window like an air gunner's target. Fantastic coincidence! There it was, like the description in my dream, neatly divided into four: North and South pulling away, East and West turning toward each other.

But . . . that's not how it happens! A thought hit me, nearly knocking me over. In human affairs, the thing goes wrong. North and South, instead of holding apart, fall in on each other and clash; and this drives a wedge between East and West.

I dressed and hurried out to the coach house. The day looked different to me than the one before: there seemed a new depth in the sky. I hoped it was not too late . . . She came right away to the door when I knocked, and she looked different too: as though she had grown older. She looked tired and stern, and had no paint on her face, except a streak of vermilion down one side of her nose.

I stood in the doorway and asked her pardon. She listened politely, her eyes on mine but strangely absent. I couldn't find forgiveness in her face, or anger, or anything at all. She had gone far inside herself, and we looked at each other across two hemispheres.

"Metternich is much misunderstood, of course. In modern

eyes he has become a symbol of conservatism at its most unpopular."

"Particularly to the young. They forget that conservatism is a treasure house – albeit an infuriatingly dusty one – of centuries of accumulated experience. A rebellious generation disregards this at its peril."

My father and the Professor were staging another little scene for my benefit. They had struck up in discreet tones across the lawn, where I was lying listening to the sea and watching the drifting clouds, adrift like me.

"They argue, rightly of course, that not all of the past is worth keeping."

"If only one could see that the conservative conserves discriminately, the reactionary indiscriminately, and the revolutionary not at all . . . thus discarding the valuable lessons of the past, along with its events."

A cloud drifts and a leaf drifts, I thought, not a man. A man moves with purpose, as the sun rises with purpose into the sky; or so it seems, though in truth it stays firmly in its place, and that is the secret of its success.

I made up my mind to tackle my parents right after dinner. My father never mentioned my career directly any more; he seemed to feel that if he took it for granted I had fallen back into line, it would make it so.

"You know, Dad, that I don't plan to follow in your footsteps." I caught them in the living room before they sat down. He stopped where he was; my mother continued slowly to her chair and stood in front of it, looking at the carpet.

"Yes, I know that, Hedleigh!" He smiled at me eagerly. He had so hoped it wouldn't surface.

My mouth felt dry and I wanted to sit down. "I mean to say, I – I want to do something of my own."

"You have only to name it, Hedleigh, and most certainly you may do it."

"Well, I . . . can't name it just yet," I said feebly.

"Unless you know what it is you may have difficulty carrying it out." He drew his pipe slowly out of his pocket; his voice was gentle and just tinged with reproof.

"I'll know what it is eventually," I said.

My mother burst out: "Or you may never know!" She walked toward me with quick little steps, her hands clutched together and thrust out at me. "You'll be one of those lost souls who never find themselves! A drifter! Your wonderful promising life all gone to waste!"

"Well now, Nora." My father sounded mildly amused. "Perhaps we needn't be as negative as all that."

"Don't do History if you don't want to," she said, ignoring him. "Do something else, do anything . . . "

"I *want* to do something!"

"Well, *what?*"

"Nora . . . " my father moved nervously to her side. And now we were all standing together, a tight little group in the big room. I was conscious of all the waste space around us.

"Go to University!" my mother pleaded, her face pale and close to mine. "You're a born teacher! You come of a family of teachers!"

"Mother, I don't want to teach!"

"*Then what is it you want to do?*"

"Well, do I have to decide this minute?"

A look of pain came over my father's face and he said plaintively: "You know, there's a terrible lack of cohesion to this argument."

My mother turned on him with a cry. "*Cohesion!*" she moaned. "It's his *life* we're deciding!"

"Well listen," I said, "I don't want my life decided here and now – that's the point. I want it *undecided!*"

At the same moment we all stepped back, moving away like the flower centre in a ballet. I seemed to see us from

85

a distance, and it struck me we looked ridiculous.

My mother too had gone into a longer perspective.

"Imagine," she said, her voice low and brooding. "She only came back this week. And now this."

She looked deeply into my eyes. I looked back into hers, and fancied I saw in them reflections of reflections from my own, like the infinite effect sometimes obtained with double mirrors.

"This hasn't anything to do with Cecilia coming back," I said.

"No," she murmured, and looked down at her hands, as they slowly untangled from each other.

We both knew it was because Cecilia had come in the first place. It was she who had put the fight in me, what little there was.

My vision lifted again. I saw that I was fighting not only my parents but all the past. And I was being blockaded by everything that had ever happened. It had been gathering momentum from the word Go, increasing as it approached me at this place in time, and having its most powerful effect in the persons of my parents. Their helplessness was as great as mine, for they too had all of it at their backs. The accumulated force was pouring into them, and there was nothing they could do but add their weight to it and pass it on to me.

At what point, I wondered, does a person break from this? Where does the strength come from to set oneself against it and strike out in a direction of one's own? My Great-great-grandfather thought he was doing it when he left England. But the past is not so easily cheated: it followed him across the ocean and kept going without missing a beat.

Now it had all fallen on me. The temptation was to simply lie down and let it roll over me and carry me along. Otherwise, I decided, you have to meet it with terrific strength, with all the force of the ages, the power of a god, and above all the fearlessness of a Man.

"What makes a man?" I asked Doctor Holtzman.

Perhaps I should have said constitutes. He laughed and said, "A woman."

"Seriously," I said. We were fishing from the sailboat, anchored a quarter-mile off the headland. It was Indian summer. And he was a man. I kept trying to analyze what it was about him. His energy perhaps? . . . that rush of life that moved everywhere with him and stayed round him, almost visibly, even out on the water. And I believed he had courage. I had heard more by then of the circumstances of his painful marriage. I had never heard him complain.

He said seriously, "I am serious."

I thought it over. Fishing is not where you draw diagrams of ideas. You let them nibble away; and when you get a real one you haul it in.

"Joy!" he said suddenly, after a long time. "A man has the capacity for joy. You can take his measure by where he finds it. Little men look for it in corners and under the carpet. Great men know it's in the air all around us." He scanned the air, his big, tough face eager, almost ecstatic. "It's in this breeze on our face. We only have to reach out and touch it." I watched him reaching. "Make contact with it once and you'll never lose it. Even when you're unhappy . . ." His eyes, with their long suffering, turned to me. " . . . you can get so your unhappiness doesn't dim your joy."

Was it that about him then? It certainly seemed he had a joy in life. Life tried to knock it out of his hand, but he only laughed and held it higher.

I inspected the sky. Soft patches of blue and white melted into each other; a watercolour sky. (Was she out somewhere nearby, painting it?) To embrace life and not to blame it, whatever it did: never to criticize or repel. Wasn't this something quite close to love?

I inquired about love.

"Love? There's too much talk about it. Love is in the air – why specify? There's more love in an atom of your eyebrow than in all the love stories ever written. That which they are talking about, my son, is biology, plain and simple. Not that biology doesn't count."

And religion? Same as love. Why specify? "If a man hasn't got religion in the soles of his feet as he walks the world, he isn't gonna take it in through his ears in sermon form. The boys in the religion department," he said, frowning into the water, "are the great barrier builders. They've been hoisting those barriers from the dawn of time, for men to climb up on and kill each other. Whereas . . . " he pushed his hat over his face and took a long breath, "the barrier between one thing and another, one being and another, is the only thing worth attacking in this world. You don't break it down with force, that's the thing."

"But listen," I said to his hat, "without this separation . . . this edge around us . . . we'd all melt into a kind of stew."

"You're getting the idea." The hat didn't move. "Now get this if you can. That dividing line . . . first you have to put it there, then you have to do away with it."

I couldn't get it. "Why?" I asked.

An hour passed, or so it seemed, the horizon waving gently up and down. A blue strip lay between the horizon and the edge of the boat. Narrow strip, wide one, narrow, wide, no strip at all.

"You get these things or you don't. They're like riddles."

I got it really. Close enough. It lay out there somewhere in that little strip, slowly surfacing. I felt I could fish it in when I really needed to.

He tilted his hat up and squinted at me.

88

I said, "It's within reach."

He sat up straighter. "Heaven is within reach of every human being," he said slowly. "The hell of it is it's harder to be a human being than anything."

Was that what it was to be a man? A human being?

"To be a man," he said, with a great haunted look upon his face, "is to be half a human being. That's all we can aim for – half." Slowly he reeled in his line, and he looked upward at the sun. "Wholeness comes. It comes. But we have to be a whole half first." He went into a deep silence.

But he would be gay again at dinner, when we lugged home our fish. It was he who taught me that true gaiety is rooted in a profound and tragic nature.

My parents would be cheerful too. They were always reassured when I was with the Doctor: they imagined him talking some sense into me. If they had known him as he was, they'd have found his view too broad for safety. He'd fooled them into believing they saw eye to eye; this was because they could fit their own philosophy into his and never suspect how much room there was left over. There was room for any opinion, as there is room in the sky for the stars. He had as it were a wide-angle lens in his eyes: three hundred and sixty degrees.

Holtzman's talks always started me thinking, in contrast to the Professor's, which numbed me. The power of thought, my father often said, is the greatest power there is; but I began to see that there are many definitions of thought. To the Doctor it meant the vital flow of free images from a mind wide open. My father, if he had inclined toward poesy, might have seen it as progress along a road already laid out, though running a high course above the land and leading to lofty peaks that touched the sky, and perhaps held it up. To Cecilia it was surely the exploration of dark places, previously unknown, full of mystery and danger

. . . and a very particular promise of reward to the persisting soul.

I saw that we each have our own approach to thought, just as we have our fingerprints and the distinguishing arrangement of our features. We are beings of sharp definition and differentiation; and with all this our great challenge is to find a meeting ground. Plainly we are held apart by the differences: yet I couldn't believe we must let go of them as the price of teaming up. There was a paradox hidden here somewhere; I sensed it had been around as long as anybody had.

It was on my mind the afternoon in that same Indian summer, when I sat with my parents at teatime on the lawn. My father was resplendent again in his white summer suit, and lay in a deck chair stroking his pipe and squinting at the sky, his face blissful with thought. My mother sat on a cushion near him on the grass, her fingers busy with a piece of needlework, cool and fresh looking in her simple sleeveless dress with garden flowers fastened at the waist. She liked to display her beautiful arms, which were round and soft, and graceful as the movements of a swan. (But a swan, I knew, can be fierce and snappish and even dangerous.) She continually glanced back and forth between my father and me, where I lay sprawled on the grass, and she looked happy as she always did when there was harmony in the air. With a passion she wanted peace; but she wanted her own way, and this, I had recently worked out, constituted her central problem.

Two incompatible needs in one human being worked the same as their existence in a society: one of them had ultimately to be submerged by the other. Through Mathilde I was aware of the French-Canadian struggle to preserve identity; not that it affected her, for she had long ago submerged herself in me. I thought of the Indians and wondered what the country might be like today if their culture had managed to survive. Might it have enriched ours? Perhaps their loss was the country's loss, and my loss too; by some strange connectedness it might account for my difficulty in . . . (my thought reached for something, wavered, and reached again) locating –

The idea fell apart and I couldn't remember what I'd been thinking. My father would say it was a failure of the lanes of logic. I rolled over onto my stomach and pressed my face into the grass. I heard a faint rumble far below and knew the tide was filling the caves, the black water rushing over where my feet had stood. It was reminding me of something. And the warm wind on my neck and elbows, it too . . . and the gulls screaming in my ears; it seemed for a moment as though all the forces of nature were focused on me. You! You!

Who, me?

Who?

"Are you reading, Hedleigh?"

She could see very well I wasn't reading.

"No."

It was her way of saying I ought to be. With a book in my hand I was fulfilling my father's wishes. But a face in the grass reveals nothing.

"Well, your tea is getting cold."

"What a glorious sky!" My father had joined the team. "Have a look, Hedleigh. Winter may be on us to-morrow, you mightn't see the sky again until April."

April! It made me yearn for . . . something. I dragged myself to a sitting position and turned my face upward. All I saw was that the seasons would change. In one year I was due to enter University and start preparing myself for life. (Cecilia was living now.)

"It's nice," I said glumly.

"You seem very discontented with everything these days, Hedleigh." My mother gave a worried laugh and pricked her finger and quickly put it to her lips.

"There is something," I said, "which is called the divine discontent. But I don't know that I qualify for that."

"Not quite," my father said dryly. "The divine discontent is a precursor to action."

"I don't see that you need to be discontented," my mother went on. "You have a wonderful life here, you always have had, and a very special education . . . " I looked at her and fixed my face politely the way she liked. She leaned toward me appeasingly. "That's because you are a special person."

"Everybody's a special person," I said, "individual."

She read a rudeness in my tone, and her cheeks grew pink.

"Perhaps," she said in a voice remote and suddenly chilled. "And that may not always be a good thing."

"What on earth do you mean by that?" I demanded. We were about to be treated to some female logic. I glanced at my father. He looked as though he'd fallen asleep.

"It *is* possible," she actually said, "to be too much of an individual."

Just at that moment, as though by some mysterious design, Cecilia appeared, strolling past on the beach below. She had her sketch pad under her arm and was looking out to sea.

I jumped up and gave a shout. "Come and have tea with us!" She looked up and stood motionless as though she hadn't understood. I picked up the teapot and waved it. Tea sloshed onto the grass, and my mother gasped, as though it had fallen on her and scalded her.

Cecilia shook her head briefly and walked on, turning the pages of her sketch book. She was in her bare feet, and wore a little skirt and halter, and her arms and legs were white from her city summer. As she faced out to sea again her hair blew straight forward from the warm strong breeze blowing off the land. It seemed that even her hair fled from us, forbidding as her manner.

Why, I wondered, does she forbid us all to come near her? Almost as I asked it an answer brushed the fringes of my mind . . . I grabbed for it; but I grabbed too hard. It was gone without leaving a trace.

Yet I turned to my mother and said with certainty: "I don't agree with you. It's not possible to be too much oneself."

"Perhaps what I meant . . . " Her eyes darted over my face, seeking approval, "is that one can express oneself . . . too freely . . . "

. . . for the comfort of others.

"Yes," I said softly, "I understand."

At that she looked more deeply worried. One could understand too much too.

But none of us understood Cecilia, who led a life apart, yet haunted all our thoughts. She went several times a week to Vancouver, where Uncle Frederick had located a teacher for her; he had issued orders that she was to be free to study, to paint, to come and go as she pleased. Her allowance was provided. She was under protection.

And more than ever she possessed her own power of protection. For one hour every evening, at dinner, I could have reached across and touched her; but no one ever had a reach like that.

My parents tried.

"Good evening, Cecilia, how's your painting coming along?"

"All right." Abruptly.

Or again: "We'd like to see your work sometime."

A pause. "Oh."

Even: "Why don't you have a little exhibition?" From my mother, sweetly.

And swiftly back: "Little? My paintings are big."

"A big exhibition then!" I watched the smile vanish from my mother's face and appear on Cecilia's.

"I might."

Conversation would have failed, except that silence was taboo, and so each night my parents filled the dinner hour with busy talk between themselves. Occasionally one of them would give me a reproachful look and I would leap in, hating myself, manufacturing words, conscious of Cecilia's greater honesty and her courage in not seeking favour. She sat as though oblivious, eating slowly and steadily until she was finished. Then she stood up and left. Sometimes my father called after her, his voice mild but meaningful: "Good-night, Cecilia!"

"Good-night." Her clear voice came wafting back, almost friendly now that she was gone.

One evening my mother turned and said grimly to my father: "She's going to have a terrible time when she gets away on her own. A person who won't put herself out to be pleasant . . . "

"Put herself out!" I exclaimed. "If you have to come outside yourself to be pleasant, what does that make you?"

She was looking at me from great wounded eyes. "I think I know what you mean by that." The hurt look was altering to something else . . .

"Now then, Nora." My father sounded scared. "He doesn't mean anything."

He was seeing, as I was, the resentment hardening her features. She observed our eyes on her, and she straightened her back and forced a smile. I watched with interest as her anger and annoyance sank down and disappeared beneath the pleasant folds of her face. I thought I detected a strange pattern. Many people had a core of hostility buried deep down under their strained and pleasant faces. They showed the light side of themselves and hid the dark. I almost wondered if Cecilia, who was all turnabout in so many ways, might not be the reverse here too. Perhaps her harshness was all on the outside, while at the centre there might even be a great and true pleasantness that no one had ever suspected.

More was suspected on the nights that she stayed over in Vancouver. Then, as I watched, pretending not to, Mathilde ostentatiously removed Cecilia's setting from the table. Her eyes and her gestures proclaimed triumphal accusation. My parents purported to look at their plates, but were watching me. Everybody was watching and waiting: for what, I didn't know. As we watched, we drifted farther apart, until it seemed to me we lived on separate islands. Instead of communicating, we sent signals to each other, and often the signals were desperate. A visit to another's island immediately took on the nature of a trespass; and so these gradually diminished.

November; and she passed her sixteenth birthday out of our sight. We all bought her a present (except Mathilde, who would not even bake a cake and so my mother had to) but she didn't come to dinner. Looking out the kitchen window I saw that the coach house was dark.

I took her gifts out there late that night. Mine was a bottle of French perfume, very expensive: a wrong choice I decided, when I found myself concealing it from my mother. The door was unlocked; I went in with my heart pounding and my palms wet, as though intending to burgle the place. I hadn't been in since the day of her return, when all had been so bright. It looked eerie now in the moonlight, alive with her presence, yet hushed and deathly still. It reeked of paint, and was populated with black shadows clustered together or standing out boldly against the moon-lit walls. A large one loomed against the easel and sent excitement chasing through me.

Here was my chance to see what she was painting . . . I groped for the light switch . . . and to see again perhaps that other one, if I could find it without disturbing any-thing. Still fumbling for the light, I peered into the strange half-darkness, standing there just inside the open door, with the cold wind on the back of my head. It was probably still in the crate, that monstrous black square in the corner. She certainly wouldn't be back: there was no bus at this hour.

I could look for hours at the portrait, and know her . . . almost as he had. I pictured again her secret self exposed . . . and saw the innocent and trusting eyes as they were fixed on him. Now in my mind they seemed fixed on me.

Gently I laid the tissue-wrapped parcels on a rocking chair and went out and closed the door. The stars glowed with particular brightness as I walked back to the house.

The next day I was on the beach chewing my pencil, scrib-bling something or other, and I happened to glance along the shore and saw her. She was just into the trees; her arm in a red shirt moved slowly, then swiftly. She seemed to be sketching.

I turned and ambled away in the other direction, cir-cling slowly back through the trees. She was absorbed in her work, and I had a knack of moving soundlessly in the forest, so I was able to get quite close without her knowing. It wasn't that I wanted to spy, but just to be near her. I couldn't help seeing that her sketch pad held an eruption of colour; yet the day was completely colourless. The ever-greens seemed washed of their pigment in the dull grey light that filtered down from a lifeless sky. The ocean was nearly black. Yet she stood there snatching up one bright crayon after another, applying them with passion and a certainty of stroke. She kept glancing up at the scene, so presumably she was basing her vision on something. I could almost see the energy crackling along her fingers; and I wondered if it might be energy itself she was portraying, something she perceived behind the outer dullness.

I drew back, afraid of being caught, and hung around in the chill. Finally she started gathering up her things, folding the sketch pad and the portable easel. Again I got that thumping in the chest, and a feeling of fear, as I manoeuvred round behind a clump of trees. I was just off the path as she came marching along it. (Cecilia never strolled or ambled.)

"Oh – hi!" I called out.

"Hello." She kept going, not even glancing at me. I realized with shame that she had known all the time I was there.

I ran a few steps and caught up with her, scuttling along beside her. She had the centre of the path and didn't budge from it, so I had to go half-sideways like a crab, scraped by low branches.

"Cecilia, listen . . . "

"Thanks for the present," she said, looking straight ahead, "if that's what you want."

"I don't want anything!"

"Oh no?" she gave a little laugh.

A sharp branch nearly took the top of my head off. I felt I was getting scalped and said desperately:

"Cecilia, what's the matter?"

"Nothing's the matter, I'm busy that's all."

"Too busy to go for a walk with me now and then? To talk a little . . . "

"Talk!" She stopped so suddenly I had to turn back to face her. "Who do you think you're kidding? I know what's on your mind and it isn't *talk!* It isn't walking either!"

So that's what she was thinking!

"No," I said. "No!" It was terrible that she should think this. The thought had never entered (never?) my mind.

"Oh yes," she said softly, her face fierce. "They say men of fifty are at the dangerous age. They're not half as dangerous as boys of sixteen!"

I reeled at the insult. I'd be seventeen in a mere two months. (Uncle Frederick, I believed, was fifty.)

"Cecilia, you're mistaken! I only want to – I mean, we used to do things together. . . . "

"The things we did then," she said, "don't interest us now."

It was true.

"They do me."

"Then there's something wrong with you." She almost smiled. Then she explained, nearly kindly: "I can't be bothered fooling around, you see Hedleigh, I have something to do." It was lit up for me, the difference between someone who has something to do, and the other who has nothing to do except covet the one with the something, perhaps for that very reason.

"I understand that," I said. I understood when I was with her, and wanted to understand more. "And there's something somewhere for me to do too."

"Well then find it." Her tone might have sounded heartless. But I knew the lighter blue, what it meant, the little warmth that softened her eyes. "When you have, we'll have something to talk about."

She turned and walked away into the grey trees, her hair springing softly as she moved.

Her hair had grown a little longer. The artificial wave had gone out of it; she hadn't put it back in, and she wouldn't, I knew. Nor the make-up on her face . . . this was all part of what they had done to her there, like the stagey manner she had first arrived with, left over from her mother.

It was as though she was tainted by the pressures and influences of people, and found her true self only when she was separated from them.

But it seemed impossible to me that she had let them influence her, even for a while. Was it conceivable that she might be fashion-able, like the rest of us?

I brooded over what she had said . . . "Find it" – find my work. How had she found hers? A wave of circumstance had swept her to Uncle Frederick, who chanced to be a painter, and by that strange accident she had found it.

But, I reminded myself, she had been searching. I would search too, I answered, if I knew where. She had searched everywhere.

Yet, do you find things where you look? Or do you trip over them in the dark? Or over clues; for perhaps we never find what we want, but only signs pointing to a final Something which, if touched, would bring everything to an end . . . all the searching and attaining.

One evening I was trying to locate an old book, and went up to the attic, and there I passed Mathilde's room. The heavy, sagging oak door had come unlatched and had swung open. I couldn't help seeing her, collapsed on her knees by the bed, her head clutched in her hands. I stood rooted there, paralyzed. She twisted round inside her long flannel nightgown and saw me.

"I'm sorry," I said, abashed.

She gave a violent tug at the gown. "Don't be sorry to see me with God. There are worse things you could see in a bedroom!"

In her incendiary state, I thought with amazement how

very like Cecilia she was. They were like each other turned inside out; made of the same cloth. But one of them loved me (if you could call it that) and the other . . .

She hoisted herself into a half-sitting position on the bed. She and the bed creaked and groaned in unison.

"Come in since you're here, and join with me."

"I wouldn't know what to say to him, Mathilde."

"Saying is not the point, the point is to listen!"

"Maybe . . . " I smiled foolishly "he wouldn't know what to say to me."

"He would know what," she snapped. "He would say what I have been saying to you all your life!"

"Then I guess I needn't stay, thanks anyway, Mathilde!" And I got out.

I remembered as I picked my way down the attic stairs how Cecilia often seemed to be listening, when there was nothing around to hear. I went out into the night and had a look at the ocean. It could barely be seen, but the roar of it filled my ears so that I couldn't think. I stopped trying to think, and let the sound pour in. I stood like a channel, allowing the sea to flow through me, until at length I felt cleansed and made smooth, as seashells are smoothed by the perpetual waters.

When I turned to go back into the house I had a new knowledge within me. It was that the sea affirms itself . . . "I" . . . with each wave it proclaims it . . . "I! I!" It leaves no doubt; and it has no doubt. And it is this that drives each of us onward, no less than the sea, the need for self-affirmation.

I thought it over as I went to bed. A question had arisen in my mind. To the extent that I affirm myself, do I not separate myself from others? It had looked simple down by the shore, but the more I tried to puzzle it out the more complex it became, until it finally slipped away altogether, leaving me alone on my island with the sea rushing around me, throwing spray into my face that tasted of tears.

Thus went the winter. Cecilia came as a guest to our table, appearing each evening out of the rain or the sleet, her eyes sometimes bright, more often inturned and brooding. Did her work absorb her so, I wondered. Or was there someone? Letters came for her, from just one person, addressed in a bold, graceful hand.

I measured the days by the dinners, which seemed the same one, endlessly repeating. The weeks slipped one into the other, while we around the oval table sat still. The crystal chandelier, sent in pieces long ago from England, hung above us, lighting our noses and knuckles and our empty talk. Sometimes I had the feeling my life was hovering like that, just above me, immobile, cut in ancient patterns by the hands of men long dead.

In March, when the rain became constant, she stopped coming for meals altogether. They'd built her a kitchenette; she took the hint. I found I was forgetting what she looked like. Yet whatever I looked at, her face was between it and me.

I went for long walks and came back soaked; but instead of going in by the front door, I always curved round the back, passing along between the coach house and the house. Cecilia's front window was usually streaked with rain and misted from the heat inside, and sometimes I saw her face, blurred and still, like a mask suspended there. Once on a hunch I glanced up toward my mother's bedroom window, at the back of the house. And there was her face too. She drew back quickly, and only her image was left, hovering as though disembodied. It was more lasting than her features themselves. I never passed there again without seeing my mother's image imprinted on that upstairs window. I didn't even have to turn my head.

I was conscious all the time of a pull between them. It was tug-of-war all over again, but with me in the middle. The strength of their tugging felt equal. Though I sensed a more active effort on my mother's part, the magnetism from Cecilia balanced it, being at once more powerful and more subtle, emanating from me, from the air around us, and could I be sure not a little from herself?

My father was patriotic, and had often talked with me about our country's internal pulls: "the two-way stretch," was Doctor Holtzman's phrase for it. French and English pulled against each other from within, and beyond was the mother country (the face at the window) conflicting with the fascination of the States. I felt an identification with history for the first time. And I realized that although some Canadians might go one way and some another, the country's basic geography stayed where it was; and that was magnificent, unique, and its own.

I went up to the tower one spring afternoon, the first time I had been alone there since knowing Cecilia. The day was very bright and clear, the sea a deep blue, almost purple. Looking down I saw my mother moving in slow motion across the lawn. Her golden head was centred in a swirl of salmon pink, her coat full-skirted and flying in the wind. I looked left toward the forest, for it struck me that Cecilia would be out on such a day. And there she was in a thinning of the trees, sitting motionless, painting probably or drawing, I couldn't tell. She was facing in my mother's direction, and my mother was moving toward her, though they couldn't see each other for the row of firs that stood between them.

Suddenly Mathilde appeared from the direction of the

front door, looking like an enormous black bird, her arms widespread, shaking a mat. She was facing the water and didn't see my mother, who had her back to her.

I felt keenly my connection with them all, and thought how strange it was that I could oversee them like this, though each thought she was alone.

I watched them, on their islands. The islands were what we stood upon, and yet they were ourselves: our lesser self upon a larger one. And then in an instant, with perfect ease, I saw a way of bridging the separation. It was that the islands should grow, until all joined and we became a mainland – still in our places, but undivided. Words of Doctor Holtzman rose up out of the sea: *You have to put it there* (the dividing line) *and then you have to do away with it.*

Put it there . . . because it is that which gives the island direction and momentum in its growth; and then do away with it. . . .

We met on a path in the forest suddenly, quite unexpectedly, in April.

"Oh!" we said together. I stood smiling at her, blinking, from surprise and from the sun that was piercing the deeply shaded air with little spears of light. One of them illumined her face. She looked serious, calm and friendly. I remembered – yes – this is the look of her. I wondered whether to turn and walk her way.

"What have you been doing?"

"Just lately?" I asked.

Her hair was almost long again, her face pale and fragile but for the definite set of the mouth.

"Anytime."

"Reading Viereck's poetry." I had the book in my hand. "And last night I was listening to Bernstein."

"I've never heard of Viereck."

103

"Peter Viereck, he's new. You've heard of Bernstein."

"I met him."

"Met him!"

"At – when I was in the States."

"What's he like?"

"What's anybody like? They're like themselves!"

She spoke impatiently. She was herself. Though we'd been so separate it seemed natural to be with her here.

"Listen," I said, "can I bring the records over tonight and play them for you?"

Her only answer was: "Bring Viereck too. Sounds as though they go together."

She had her sketch book with her, and she gave me a slow little wave with it, and a smile, as she went on past.

The sun and new growth go together, and certain people and certain times. All that is divided comes together in the end, and perhaps has not even separated but only seems so. The thought formed, whole and clear, the Idea of Union, as I walked back toward the house. I was hurrying, though there was nothing waiting for me there. It was waiting behind me; moving away as I went from it; yet the movement was forward and toward. I looked out across the water and saw the sky bend low and the ocean rise to meet it.

I saw this, and saw that love is its own opposite, which is love also.

The last of the day fell in a shaft from the skylight, and mingled with dust particles (she was still no great duster) and met the fading light from the window. The effect was as a column of smoke, with music threaded through it. It seemed I watched the music and heard the light.

Afterwards I read to her, still sitting on the floor, while

she sat on the sofa, straining forward, as though she were seeing the words too in the air.

> After eight thousand years among the stars,
>> A sudden wistfulness for August
>> Tugged me – like guilt – through half a cosmos
>> Back to a planet sweet as canebrake,
>> Where winds have plumes and plumes have throats,
>>> Where pictures
> Like "blue" and "south" can break your heart with sweet
>> suggestiveness.

> After a mere eight flickers, nothing changed there
>> Among the birds, still just as blazing,
>> Among the rain of leaves on rivers,
>> The heartbreak of the south and blue,
>> The canebrake-sweet of August night;
>>> But only
> The people changed, my people, oh my people, my
> forgetters.

> After eight cycles, how is this you greet me?
>> Where is my horse? Where is my harp?
>> Why are the drums of goat-skin silent?
>> Spin my abyss of resin-wine;
>> Drape me my cloak of prophecy;
>>> My name is . . . .
> And then I said the true and lost and terrifying word.

But not a word had she to say about the poems or the music, and I saw that she was right: that these could not be improved upon by the addition of our paltry opinions.

The quiet deepened around us with the darkness. I had often planned what we might talk about if we ever got together; but instead I grasped the Idea behind communication. You talk mainly to bridge a gap, that gulf which separates people and fills them with fear. We seemed to have no need of it, but sat listening to the night sounds and remembering many things. The wind was singing round the corners of the building, punctuated now and then by a faint scratching as a small animal scampered over the doorstep. In the distance the sea affirmed itself.

She didn't turn on a light, but stayed where she was on the sofa, surrounded by the cushions and the debris; and with the vanishing light the disorder around her disappeared, leaving only her outline. Then that too blended into the night . . . and only her presence remained, and filled the room.

When it was time for me to go, she moved silently to the door and opened it. I following, stumbling over a few books and some shoes. I heard her soft laugh. Her face in the shadow was friendly . . . perhaps a little more. I had already kissed her once or twice. It was time.

The words came the next day. We walked for miles through the forest, then threw ourselves down on the grass of the hills and talked as though we'd been stopped up for many lifetimes.

I heard about her mother's death, and told for the first time to anyone about the doll my father took away from me.

"The soldiers," I told her, "are still in their box somewhere. Maybe they're saving them for my son."

"Oh." She laughed, waving one foot lazily at the sky. "Are you going to have a son?"

"I suppose so. They're going to want grandchildren like crazy."

"Me," she said, throwing back her head, half sitting up

and leaning backwards on her elbows, "I'm going to have a daughter."

"How do you know?"

"I just know." Slowly she sat up. "It's one of the things I know."

She stared down at the earth on which we were sitting, and I was reminded that it was the same earth we had walked on when she announced she was going to learn everything.

"It is hard," I said, looking at her and wondering, as I had always wondered, "to find things out."

"That's true." She glanced at me quickly. "The things you don't want to know, everybody's pushing. And what your whole soul is dying for, you have to . . . " she stretched her fingers taut "dig for! Like jewels . . . " her fingers slowly clawed the soil "buried in the earth." She continued after a pause. "What do you think is the reason for that?"

"I – I don't suppose there's a reason," I said.

"That shows how much you know!" Again I heard the taunting voice of her childhood. "There's a reason for everything."

I felt uneasy, and so I teased her. "You sound like my father. He's great on reason."

"There are two different kinds of reason," she said, and leaping to her feet half slid down the hill to the beach and ran away. I had said something to end our closeness, but didn't know what. Yet, as she reached the end of the beach, just before it curved into the black trees, she turned and waved. I jumped up, wondering if she was beckoning. But my better sense told me merely to wave back.

The next day she showed me her paintings, setting them up on the easel one by one. I had expected a great surprise, some sort of revelation. But as I looked at them, at the brave colours and bursts of energy, the mysterious patterns that seemed to be guarding a secret while revealing its essence, I simply recognized them.

"I like them," I said.

She nodded and started putting them away. She'd have despised me for studious comments on her brushwork.

Feeling quite at ease, I said, "I think I might like to write."

She looked over her shoulder, while stacking the paintings against the wall. "You could be good."

"What makes you think so?" I was surprised.

"It showed in your letters."

"All those letters you never answered!" She was on her way back to me; I reached out and gave her a gentle poke in the ribs. She caught my hand, and we wrestled a little, laughing. But she stopped, her face half turned from me, and an air of seriousness about her that stopped me too. I was still holding her by the wrists.

She said something in a tone so low I couldn't catch it; but it contained the name Frederick. I just saw the clear edge of her profile, tilted down and away, with her hair falling toward it, and saw her lips move, slowly, as though numbed.

"It only happened the once. I didn't realize at first what he . . . until – "

"Yes," I said quickly, "yes, I know. . . . Never mind. The bastard!" I was furious and scowling, but full of happiness. I slid my arm around her waist, but she ducked away and picked up the next painting and carried it across the room.

"Actually," I said, after a silence, "I've written a story."

She hesitated for a second, not turning to me, then said casually: "Bring it over tonight and read it to me." She went on lifting the paintings and setting them down in a neat stack against the wall.

I went over in such a hurry after dinner I nearly forgot to take the story, and had to rush back for it. She was waiting for me, looking no different than usual though the whole world had altered. Everything had come to life in a strange way. Everything except my story; as I read it aloud it slowly died, beginning immediately after the title, "The Island."

She listened, hunched up on the sofa, hugging her knees, her face lowered onto them. As the pages fell and she didn't move, I felt I stood before the Bar of Judgement. All the words were in the wrong places and they were no good anyway. I croaked to a halt and waited, full of despair.

She lifted her head and only said, "It's good." I stared at her in the small glow of the single lamp that burned between us, and saw something in her eyes that I had never seen there before. Admiration. I was not sure I had seen it anywhere, turned in my direction. It wasn't necessary to a parent's love. But I realized in an instant that it was essential to a woman's.

Her approval flowed toward me like a bridge spanning the space between us. On it I travelled to her, turning out the light on my way. Her face disappeared, then began to glow softly as I held it between my hands. We whispered and kissed, and soon were wrestling, laughing, preparing for a new encounter, old as our beginnings. It had been in the planning as long as we had been ourselves.

I found her in the dark. I had never lost her; always we had been connected at the centre, sharing the same nature. And the nature of ourselves, though it was flesh, was also bliss.

Crowned with radiance though we might be, our toes were stubbed on myriad articles of junk littering the sofa. We were crowded on all sides by papers, paint brushes, books. I even detected the rattle of a cup and saucer. I sat up at one stage and swept the whole lot of them off in a fury, in a mighty raging joy, and her peal of laughter mingled with the crash.

"You're demolishing my house!"

"I'll demolish you!" I cried and fell upon her like a very house. But I was careful to stay just this side of demolition, where life lay at its peak.

And when at the end, which was also the beginning, we lay crumpled and warmly together, I was absolutely certain that the perfect, the flawless, happiness could never be lost.

"Say," I said suddenly, "did you really like my story?"

"I like you better." She touched the tip of my nose with hers.

"You'd better," I said and grasped her familiarly. For there was no separation now between us or any of earth's things.

I got up very early the next morning and went outside. There was a pale, gentle light over everything, softening the edges of the treeline and the shore, and behind me the mountain. For I stood slowly turning, taking in everything. My body felt light and clear, and my mind at peace with a certain knowledge. It was that love filled the world, every atom of the world and all human beings, whatever their actions. They were moved and motivated by love: by love working rightly or love gone wrong; but by nothing beyond this, for beyond this there was nothing.

She had told me to come over after supper. I put in the day, wondering what she could possibly be doing. The hours to me were endless. I thought she might be planning some surprise, a special meal, or dressing herself with particular care, as I had heard women do when they're in love.

When I got there she was painting. She merely looked up and faintly smiled and turned right back to her canvas.

"Here I am," I ventured to say after about five minutes.

"I see that," she murmured, and went on painting.

I stood in the grey light, waiting.

"I want to use the last of the light."

I said with a try at a laugh, "What's the matter? Do you think there won't be another day?"

"Do *you?*" She threw the words sharply over her shoulder, while her brush paused and then drove on.

I wandered away and sat in a chair by the window, where I watched the day coming to an end. I pondered gain and loss; they are considered opposites, two different things, yet I saw that one was contained within the other.

She didn't make a sound as she came up behind me, but I knew she was there and I didn't turn.

"Here I am," she said, using my same words, mocking me a little.

Here she was, for it was in this direction she'd been moving since we met. Now that she was here, where would she move next? It was not in her nature to stand still.

I swung around and buried my face in her stomach, gripping her by the waist. She stroked my hair with slow and gentle fingers, and I thought she sighed.

"The ocean," I said teasingly, "still batters the earth."

We were up on the headland, in the very same place. She gave me a quick look, remembering. She was lying on her side, propped up on one elbow, her hair flowing over her shoulder and onto the earth. I ran my fingers through it, blue-black and soft and sweet; then bent my head and slipped it through my mouth.

"Salt and sweet," I murmured. "The only two tastes. You taste of them both."

"Sweet and sour, I thought more like." She made a little face at me.

"No. Sour is artificial. An absence of sweet. The way, for instance, evil is an absence of good."

She sat up quickly, her hair sweeping my face like a rush of cobwebs.

"Do you really think . . . " she gazed down at me with a penetrating look, her face veiled by a slight smile, "that evil is only an absence of good?"

I saw a memory present in her eyes. I had had a dream, but couldn't remember it. And once, with her, I had touched certain depths. Today we sat in the sunshine, far from everything, close to the centre of happiness. But a great war lay behind us; Nazi hands were still dripping blood. Had they demonstrated a mere absence of kindness? Doctor Holtzman was a Jew. Think . . . if he had been German.

"I suppose not," I said and reached for her, but she drew away.

I had hoped we might be light-hearted. But though her step was light, and her touch, there was a deep centre in her, perpetually activating, and containing knowledge of dark things.

Yet it almost seemed that by that depth might be measured the height of the joy.

It was this: this was the joy Doctor Holtzman meant when he said, "in the air all around us. Make contact with it once and you'll never lose it."

"Who are you talking to in there?" Mathilde stretched her busy neck into my room.

"I am talking to myself!" I said with dignity.

She laughed, a frown between her eyes. "Tell yourself

then for me, you will starve yourself into a grave in one more week."

"There are other things in this world, Mathilde" – I broke it to her gently – "besides food. Man does not live by bread alone."

"Man does not live long without it," she snapped.

"The length of a life is not the measure of it." I didn't want to insult her, but there it was. Length of life she had, but had she ever held love in her arms? I looked at her withered body, crouched in the doorway; she had been the same as long as I had known her. My mother each year was a little altered, and so was my father. But Mathilde didn't change at all. She had passed beyond it and simply endured, like the aged pines outside the window.

Yet ought not love to endure like that?

"Come in, Mathilde," I said. She hobbled toward me. I took her arm and looked into her face, seeing in it a kind of beauty – for she was faithful. She looked back at me, blinking, tears standing in her eyes; and both of us were too full of love for words.

"What are you thinking?"

She'd been sitting forever in silence, tracing a pattern in the earth with her fingertip.

She raised her eyes but didn't answer. It was afternoon, late in a warm, heavy-scented day. We were up on the headland.

"Cecilia?"

"Do you know how many times you've asked me that today?" she said.

"And do you know how many times you haven't answered?"

She flopped out full length on her back and closed her

eyes. "What I am thinking," she said, "can't be told."

"I'll tell you what I'm thinking."

"Must you?" She laughed, looking up at me through two slits in her eyes.

"Don't you want to hear that I love you?"

"Definitely not!" The eyes flew open.

I searched her face. Her mouth had gone stern.

"But Cecilia . . . "

"Listen!" She lifted up on one elbow. "Anyone who can talk can say I love you! What a word . . . I wish it had never been invented. Think how wonderful it'd be if we didn't have the word and had to convey it some other way!"

It made me wonder if she hadn't spent too much time alone. I sat brooding and looking out at the sun as it inched down toward a long grey cloud resting almost on the water. I could feel the heat going out of the day.

She stood up; I sensed her eyes on me and glanced upward. Her face was in shadow, the sun outlining her shoulders and arms. Her hands were lightly on her hips.

"If you really want to know," she said, "I love you better than they do."

She turned and walked away, carefully placing her feet along the tip of the slope. I was too stunned to follow her. I watched until she started down the hill, and saw her body slowly disappear, from the feet upward, like the cat in Wonderland.

Beyond her the sun was just disappearing over the water, sinking behind a long cloud. In the instant before its light vanished, it blazed forth like an enormous diamond; its rays shot off in all directions, a full circle of blinding white light filled with colour. Then it was gone and the ocean was dull grey without a trace of the brilliance which, after all, had been only illusion.

"If you love me," I said to her that night, "then why . . ."

"Shhh," she said, and kissed me.

I forgot what I'd been going to say. At the same time everything became very clear. There was nothing at all to worry about. The confusions and inequalities existed only when we stood apart. Together we were one whole being with no division line. I was myself, and not only myself but her also, and the total of us was immense.

At night or in the early morning we swam on the far beaches, naked as we had never dared to be in childhood. But our shrieks of laughter must have awakened memories in the moon.

It was only with the day that shadows appeared beneath her eyes, and the seriousness in her voice. And she would go about her work. While I . . .

Whenever I went to the coach house I found her painting.

"Don't you ever get tired of that?"

Her face bright with amazement, she asked: "Tired of it? Painting? . . . Do you get tired of yourself?"

"Yes . . . " And of the writing I tried to do and couldn't, because my mind strayed to her, or never left her.

"Hmmm." She looked me over with an air of knowing.

I felt I mustn't blame her if she tired of me sometimes too.

After that I tried not to disturb her but let myself in quietly and waited. I was never sure whether she knew I was there or not.

One day she said, her back to me, "Haven't you something you want to do?"

"Yes," I said, "but I can't do it while you're painting."

She laughed. "You could. You could very well. I'm not the only fish in the sea."

"But you are," I stammered. "You are to me. Does that mean I . . . I'm not the only fish to you?"

Again that look, seeming to say "You poor fish." She came to me and kissed me, but I was remembering the look. The looks she gave me sprang from depths far greater than her actions. For she was made up of many layers; and the one I could laugh with and hold in my arms was the least of her. The others went through and beyond her and made up the Otherness I had seen in her the first day.

Perhaps, I thought, we were all like this, but were insulated from our Otherness. I suspected the reason: that with our surfaces we could meet, but in our depths we were too far apart and could not endure the distance.

I considered the uneasiness that had prevailed around our dinner table in the days when she had joined us there. And I'd asked her recently (being worried about my parents, their reaction to her, and the future): "Couldn't you try to be polite to them, Cecilia?"

"Polite?" She was astonished. "I'm always polite to them." I could see that she believed it. "Why, I'm never rude, am I? Tell me when I was rude!"

I marvelled at her innocence. And at once I saw the reason for her silences at dinner. When we spoke she didn't hear us: she was listening to the Other. It made a stronger bid for her attention than we could do.

Thinking of this, I noticed that my parents' hints were thickening the air. University Entrance time was looming. There was an illusion of theirs that I had to dispel.

I tackled them at breakfast on a rainy day. There was no right time for this, and I thought the darkness of the morning might provide relief. When my father was into his third cup of tea, I said cautiously:

"I've been thinking . . . I might like to be a writer."

"A writer!" they both exclaimed.

My father set his cup down and said, with evident joy, "But that's excellent! You can do English! They've a splendid course . . . " His eyes were positively dancing. He turned to my mother in excitement. "It's perfectly natural," he told her. "He comes by it honestly . . . "

"A writer!" she said again, staring at me in amazement. "Why, I can't get him to write a simple thank-you note."

"I don't want to write thank-you notes," I said.

"Oh, you're going to be one of those *artists*," she said sarcastically, "who work at their own whim."

"Nora, please!" Those words were his way of saying shut up. She got the message and her eyes flashed.

"Now then, Hedleigh . . . " he turned to me. "Let's work this out."

"There isn't anything to work out, Dad. I don't feel I can benefit from University English. I don't aspire" – I essayed a smile – "to write an *Iliad*."

There was a short silence.

"Presumably," he said coolly, "you would find it useful to know English."

"I know English," I said. "What I want to know is – life."

"Oh my God." He turned his face sharply away from me.

My mother uttered a short, shrill laugh. "I would have thought," she said swiftly, "you were getting some of that right here."

There was a little pulse beat in her neck, where the veins were taut, pulled tight by the sudden upthrust of her head. Her mouth was drawn back and slightly open, like the mouths of those in great pain or newly dead. The deep reality of the moment showed me that such levels were touched only sparingly, and that most of her reactions – like anyone's – came from much closer to the surface.

"Well then." My father spoke in a measured voice. "How did you have in mind to proceed?"

"I haven't worked that out. I was thinking first of where

I want to get to." I imagined I saw him wince at the preposition.

"I take it then," he remarked, "that you are still open to reason."

"I doubt it. If reason means four years at University."

"Many writers, Hedleigh, spend four years – and four times four – writing things that end up in the waste basket."

"And as likely as not," I replied, "they had their training in a classroom, picking Virgil apart."

"What on earth would you write about?" my mother asked incredulously. I kept my face straight and assured her I would think of something.

"The technique alone," she said, "takes years to develop."

"Then I'd better get started," I replied. "It's like planting young trees . . . "

"I thought I had planted a young tree." Her voice was tragic, her profile purposely appealing; she had surfaced, after her true feeling of a few moments before. "And I thought it would become an oak, strong and deeply rooted."

I glanced at my father. His face wore a look of sufferance. We almost smiled at each other.

"I dreamed of it bearing fruit . . . "

"Nora . . . " he broke in quietly. "This may not be the best time for poetic indulgence."

She gave him a look and stood quickly and left the room.

"For God's sake, Hedleigh," he burst out, "just don't write poetry!" And then we did smile, we couldn't help it.

I reported back to Cecilia.

"They want to know what I'll write about."

"Well?" she asked. "What will you?"

"Love, I suppose."

"Everybody writes about love."

"And knows nothing about it."

"Do you?" she inquired, after a pause.

"I hope so." I patted her bottom.

She was silent for another moment. "I hope so too," she said, but with her words was a deep look, a strange look, which set off a warning note in me.

Yet the bomb, when it fell, fell out of the blue, as bombs do. We were lying face up on the beach, our eyes closed, holding hands. The sun was burning through our brown skins, bleaching our bones white. I felt her hand tense a little, and I squeezed it back. She said:

"You know I plan to study Art, don't you?"

"Well, I knew you . . . were keen on it . . . "

She laughed a little and drew her hand away, shading her eyes with it as she turned to me.

"Keen," she said. "I love your words."

"What's wrong with keen?"

"Nothing." She spoke abruptly. "I'm keen to go to Montreal."

"To – Montreal?" I stared into her face which was streaked with sand and salt. "What do you mean?"

"I mean I'm going there in the fall."

I pushed myself up by my elbows. She had closed her eyes again. "What about us?"

"Oh, I don't know." She sounded vague. "That'll sort itself out."

"Sort itself out?" My head throbbed and I felt dizzy.

"We have to take things one at a time."

"But . . . did you say study Art? You have an art teacher now!"

"No I haven't."

"In Vancouver . . . !"

"That isn't . . . " she stopped.

"Not a teacher?"

"Not – art." There was a strange reserve in her voice.

"What is it then? What are you saying?"

Stillness enveloped her. She had said enough.

"My God, Cecilia, Montreal! All that way? At your age . . . "

She laughed and sat up quickly in a spurt of sand.

"I seem to be old enough to suit you at other times!"

I put my hand on hers. "Celie, you can't, you just can't."

"Let go of my hand," she said very quietly. The iron had come into her voice.

"I wasn't going to restrain you by force!" My laugh was shrill, hurting my ears. Inwardly I was cold and burning. Here I was giving up my education for her, and she wasn't even willing to – "But you don't like living in cities, you told me that, don't you remember? And have you considered whether that's the best city anyway? It all depends on the teacher you get . . . "

She broke in. "When you're all through presenting your case . . . "

"It's your case I'm presenting!"

"You're *talking* about me, you're *concerned with yourself!*"

I had a brainwave. I jumped up, grinning, and pointed a finger in her face:

"*To the tower!*"

She gave me a long look and slowly stood.

"*You* go to the tower," she said. "And maybe you'll bump your head on the sky and get it circulating."

She walked away into a cloud of gulls that were drifting above the land, ominously waiting. My facial expression felt strangely like my father's as I watched her go, and the frantic beating of my heart closer perhaps to my mother's.

120

She made no mention of it for several days. I hoped she had forgotten. But then she burst out with:

"I can't stand your eyes!"

"My eyes? What's the matter with my . . . "

"They pull at me! You come over here and I can feel your eyes before I even hear your steps. They're like an animal's . . . beseeching – there! They're doing it now!"

"You're imagining things!" I protested.

"Here!" She ran and snatched up a hand mirror from her dresser. "Look for yourself." She pushed it into my hand.

I looked at my eyes in the mirror. "They look all right to me." I had a pimple on my left cheek. If I was looking anxious it was because of that.

But the way she watched my eyes, it got that the very sight of her filled me with dread.

Finally I came up with a solution.

"Cecilia, if you'll move to Vancouver and study there, I'll go to University."

She was painting as I said it. I was quite at home with her back. She laid down her brush and turned to me.

"That," she said, "is a fine reason for going to University."

"Show me a better one," I said bitterly. "You've been telling me for years it's crazy to lock oneself up in study. Now you're proposing to do just that."

"I didn't say anything about locking myself up."

"No! You're going to be free as a bird, I can see!"

She started walking slowly toward me. "You don't want me to be free, is that it?"

There was a deadly quality in her voice.

"No, no . . . I mean yes – Oh Celie, I only mean – Do you mean then you can be happy without me?"

"Happy! Happy!" she burst out. "Oh, you!"

She stood there shaking her head slowly, gazing at me with pity and sorrow and a touch of amusement. I saw with a wild hope that the love was not entirely gone after all. She reached out a hand tenderly and I grabbed her in my arms and thought I heard against my shoulder, "You just don't know anything."

But it was only another of her statements, and they were all a mystery to me. The way, when I said, "What about that daughter we're going to have?" she answered, laughing, "Who said *we*?" Then immediately she was serious: "I think you were probably right when you said you'd have a son. I can picture you with a son."

"Can you?" And I grinned at her to hide my fear. "We could have one of each."

"No," she said slowly. "I think I am only going to have one girl. I think you will have a son and I'll have that girl."

It was eerie: she spoke of that girl as though she already knew her.

"Well, it may be a little early to settle it," I said.

"Yes, or . . . " Her voice dropped low as she turned away, and I thought she may have said, "or a little late."

And it was in the same tone, half-heard or maybe half-imagined, that she finished a sentence:

" . . . my friend from Vancouver."

The words came out of nowhere, cutting across some brooding thought of mine.

"To see you . . . did you say? . . . here?" (He of the beautifully inscribed letters!)

She nodded, her face eloquent and secret.

"Okay," I said vigorously, "fine, if you say so."

She gave me a curious look and smiled. I tried to smile back, but she looked away and the effort was wasted.

She later put me out of my misery (did she know?) by

mentioning that her friend was a woman. But when it developed she was an Indian, I was torn with anxiety again. What was she doing befriending an Indian? I would not have put it past her to join the tribe . . . and appear before my family in war feathers, when they'd been two hundred years living this down.

On the evening in question, hearing the car, I edged out into the driveway, in hopes of being introduced to the squaw. The big black Buick slid slowly past our house and rounded the drive to the back. I remarked to myself how some of them had come up in the world, even if they did lose the country.

The coach house door was just out of my sight. Cecilia's voice was welcoming as I had never heard it before; it sounded gay and young as it mingled with the slow deep tones of the woman. I eased round the corner of the house, hoping Cecilia might wave me over; but they'd already gone inside. Obviously I was not being invited to dinner.

After our own dinner, over which there hung a peculiar silence, I took up a position in the upstairs hall. I watched out a back window next to my mother's bedroom, and again was uneasily aware of a certain identification with her. Cecilia and friend emerged about eight o'clock. The first thing that struck my eye was the sari. *That* kind of Indian! I immediately felt more respect: she was from farther away.

I hurried downstairs again. They were headed toward the beach and might ask me to join them on their walk. Cecilia must have seen me as she went past: I was posted in plain view on the edge of the lawn, and she was facing me, talking to the woman, who had her back to me. The foreigner was tall and imposing and held Cecilia firmly by the arm as though steering her. Cecilia looked frail and delicate in her grip. She was wearing one of her American dresses; these she put on for nobody, least of all for me, and the sight of it filled me with alarm. Something was happening to influence her again.

They went off down the beach, walking close together by the edge of the water, which was on its way out. The woman's robe, of a strong blue shade, billowed and swayed around her, giving her the appearance of additional life. Above it her hair gleamed very black, wound up in a high nest. The same gleam shone delicately over the landscape. The day had been sultry, and a fine dampness was spread over everything, making it look as though the tide had receded from the whole land. The sky was a mass of foaming clouds, and the sea was still.

Mathilde came up behind me; I heard the beads before the furtive footfall.

"What is this?" she asked. "Who is that down there?"

"Cecilia," I said coolly. "And a friend." I continued to treat her to my back.

"You are not walking with them?" And she added in a tender tone, "mon petit."

"What would I have to say to them?" I didn't dare turn now.

She laid a claw on my shoulder for an instant and left me alone. Why doesn't love, I wondered, come from the right direction? (I had forgotten for the time that it comes from every direction; and hadn't yet discovered that the only failure is a failure in connection.)

They were far in the distance, but their talking could fairly be seen. I watched them until not even their walking could be seen, but only their dwindling. They became two dots at the end of the narrow yellow strip of sand where it disappeared in a point: then a single dot standing still. But I knew it was moving inexorably away from me.

Like this, I thought, we are all moving away from each other . . . an expanding universe on earth.

The next day it came out. The woman, whose name was Madame Bashir, was the person she had been studying with: probing, as she put it, the mysteries.

"What mysteries?" I asked, completely mystified.

She laughed, and that was her sole answer.

"You're a mystery yourself," I said.

"Then," said she softly, "you should study me."

"I would like to."

"Not really. Not to know me."

From there on, as she talked, I didn't understand her. She used words I had never heard before. The little book she had once treasured and carried around with her came up for mention and was called, apparently, a *gita*.

"Why wouldn't you ever let me see it?" I asked.

"An intellectual like you?" she laughed. "You'd have scoffed."

"What are you talking about? I'm no intellectual." But I was flattered to be called one, which proved that I had the makings. "Well I wasn't one then."

"You were a worse one then. You've improved."

"Well let me see it now," I said.

"You haven't improved that much."

It seemed this was related to her decision to go to Montreal.

"My destiny is there."

"What makes you think this?" I asked.

"It's in my palm."

"Your palm!?" Now I was the one to laugh, and she was serious. "My God, Cecilia! This is the twentieth century!"

"Thanks for telling me." There was fury in her eyes, some dark force arising as she said: "There are forces. . . ."

Forces were threatening to sweep us away . . . from our love and each other. . . .

"Listen to me, Cecilia . . ."

" . . . forces beyond our control – "

"We control our own lives!"

"Yes, we must."

"Then why are you saying – "

"We have to meet these forces, and know them, and work with them or against them, depending on which kind they are."

"Which . . . which kind?"

"Good or evil."

We stared at each other; I recalled that she had been steered toward this by Frederick, our uncle, who was both good and evil.

Yet it had always been in her . . . with her signs and portents. *I'm a Scorpio.* I was finding out what it meant.

"Cecilia," I said very quietly. "If your aim is the study of painting, then say so. Let's discuss the thing on that level. That I can understand. My mother is artistic too . . . ."

"Artistic!" She snorted.

"Yes! Artistic! What do you mean by that?"

"Your mother," she said grimly, "is a piddling little dilettante on a string."

I was speechless. She marched over to her palette and stirred the colours to a mud. I watched as their brightness sank in and was lost. Yet when she applied a few careful strokes to her canvas, it miraculously heightened the pure reds and purples that were there. She liked those royal colours. Personally they hurt my eyes.

Wounded to the quick I said: "This woman has cast a spell on you! You're bewitched!"

She laughed and gave a wiggle of her hips and a saucy flourish of her brush in the air.

I felt totally defeated. There was no way I could catch hold of her. An idea that had been in the back of my mind since she mentioned Montreal came forward. Humiliated, I said, "If you're absolutely determined to go to Montreal, how would it be if . . . if I come too?"

There was silence. Her brush traced a slow steady line.

"I can't stop you if you want to move to Montreal," she said with reserve.

"Does that mean you don't want me?"

"Oh want you, *want you!*" She swung on me, flinging down her brush in a fury.

I broke in, "I only mean . . . " then finished lamely, "maybe my destiny is there too."

Her mouth fell open. We stood like two stones for a second, then both started laughing. And I said, "Do you want to know why I used to call you Sandy? Because you were like sand in the spinach!"

She gave a shriek and fell into my arms.

"Well now you can call me Spinach! I've still got the grit, but you like to eat me up!"

A little more grit than usual was called for as I headed toward my father's study. Yet I felt less reluctance than at other times; there was a greater fear behind me than ahead.

"Come in, Hedleigh." He stood up, smiling, looking like someone from another world. It was true that I had been living between two worlds, my parents' and Cecilia's. With my parents I lived on one plane only; while with Cecilia I slipped into other dimensions. The main trouble, for all of us, was synchronizing the lanes.

I thought I'd better take it from the ground up, so began by telling him I was in love with Cecilia. This he knew anyway, or he knew I was sleeping with her: I couldn't have said whether or not he equated the two.

He accepted the announcement calmly . . . with an effort. And right away he began:

"Love is important, Hedleigh. But it's not the whole of life."

"I think it is, sir." I always used sir when I saw we were

worlds apart. It separated us further, which is probably what I wanted.

"Well, whether it is or not," he said patiently, "I don't suppose you came in here to have a debate about the tender passion, so-called."

"No sir, I didn't."

"Then why don't you skip the preliminary and get to the point." He smiled helpfully.

"Because I – " a slight faintness came over me. I hadn't expected to be rushed. "I thought Mother ought to hear the later part too. The preliminary was just for you." I smiled back at him, but he was already on his way to the door, where he called out in a commanding voice: "Nora! Nora, will you come here, please? Hedleigh has something he wants to tell us!"

What's the hurry, I thought desperately. The preliminary would have settled his nerves. I'd even planned to offer him a drink. I had a small flask in my pocket, which I'd been saving for just such an occasion.

My mother came in looking scared. The sight of her frightened me to death.

"What's the matter?" she demanded.

"Nothing!" I said cheerfully, my voice breaking in two places. "Why is everyone always apprehensive when a person simply wants to say something?"

"What is it you want to say?" She stayed planted just inside the doorway.

"Well, sit down, for pete's sake!"

"Is it that bad?"

My father laughed, and this broke the tension. I went to her smiling, and led her by the arm across the room. Her arm felt frail and thin and she moved reluctantly.

"I only want to mention that Cecilia and I . . ." my voice seemed to dry up for a second. My father said bluntly, "Hedleigh and Cecilia are in love."

My mother pulled her arm out of my grip with amazing speed and strength. She drew back and faced me, and said violently, "But you're related!"

"Everybody is related!" I said. "She's not my sister – she's not even my cousin. Victoria and Albert . . . "

"All right!" My father cut in forcibly. "Let us not come to blows!" He rounded on my mother. "He's in love with Cecilia and that's that. At least it's out in the open. Now we'll go on from there!"

"You're not going to marry her!" she burst out at me.

"Are you telling me or asking me?" I was starting to feel hot behind my ears.

"She is asking you," my father said with extreme calm. "And you don't have to answer."

My mother seemed to leave us, travelling inward and saying softly to herself, "I knew . . . I knew . . . "

She had known long before I did. I looked at her bright head, bowed, blond as ever, but wondered: did she bleach it now? Why does a woman hang on like this – my thoughts wandered – to her youth?

"All right, Hedleigh." My father addressed me with quiet command. "Let's have it."

"Cecilia wants to study Art in Montreal."

My mother lifted her head. "She's going to Montreal?"

I said curtly, "She may."

"When?" she asked sharply, her voice escalating with hope.

My control snapped. "Well, don't be in too much of a hurry, Mother! Because when she goes I'm going with her."

Well then there was a silence and a half. The room was so quiet I heard the sound of Mathilde in the hall clapping her hand over her mouth.

Finally my father broke the tension, saying gently,

"Rather a heartless way to impart such a piece of intelligence."

"I *did* have a preliminary prepared!" I felt deeply wronged.

"And what," he asked, "are you going to do in Montreal while Cecilia is studying? What are *you* going to study?"

"I don't know."

"How are you going to keep yourself?"

I knew this was coming.

"I'll get a job."

"What kind of a job?" *"A job doing what?"*

They both spoke at once. I cried out, "You're both speaking at once!"

"We are saying the same thing!" my father shouted. "And I ask it again! What job? You're seventeen years old and you don't know how to do a damn thing!" He moved toward me, peering as though having trouble seeing me. "You are planning to follow that girl all across the country? How are you travelling? On your hands and knees?"

No, I thought, on my belly. I wanted to knock him down.

"Listen, Dad, I know how it looks . . . "

"Oh *you do!* You're intelligent enough to know that!" He turned with a bright idiotic smile to my mother, who said in a tense voice, "Couldn't she study Art in Vancouver?"

Oh yes, I thought bitterly, now it's a different tune! Once you wished her in Timbuktu! She's a pawn to you – move her here, move her there, ship her to Baltimore, chuck her out into the coach house, snatch her back from Montreal where she wants to go – all because of how it relates to me!

"No," I said, trying to sound friendly, "no, she can't . . . I – I've been through this with her. You see, she has a friend, an Indian." To my father, "From India. Not our kind." Then quickly to my mother, knowing what women are, "A woman!"

"And?" my mother asked icily. "What about this woman?"

"Well she . . . " and now I was really embarrassed. "She thinks Cecilia's got a . . . some kind of a destiny in Montreal."

"A *what?*" my father asked bitingly.

I was sore and said loudly, "Destiny! Lots of people believe in it. In the East – "

"And in the West we believe in common sense! But if you want to talk about destiny, very well. What kind of destiny is waiting there for *you!* They wouldn't even have you as a street cleaner, you've got no muscle!" He looked me up and down with contempt. Then his lips curled in a little smile. "Or perhaps Cecilia will sell some paintings – though I seriously doubt it – and you'll live off her!"

I looked down at my shoes. There was no sound but my mother's breathing and that of the sea. My own seemed to have stopped.

My father's voice continued at last, very quietly. "It seems to me I have heard some talk from you about – manliness. You have quite properly concerned yourself with its definition."

I felt the outline of the whisky flask against my hip. I hated the stuff. I couldn't hold it and didn't want to. And every time my mother had thanked her stars that I was not of military age, I had silently echoed it. I didn't want to go out onto a battlefield and die, perhaps slowly, in pain. It was better to live in pain.

"A man is many things, Hedleigh. To a woman he is strength. He represents leadership. He is worth following – if only to guide a woman in her rightful direction. Look at me, Hedleigh. Lift your eyes, son."

I lifted my eyes to his in shame. There was water between us; he shimmered and blurred.

"A man does not . . . " with slow emphasis "follow."

And I heard her voice again, from years ago. *You should go your own way, and make me follow if I'm going to, or let me not, but not follow me.*

I don't care, I thought. I said to him, "I don't care." I turned to my mother. "I don't care what it looks like or what anyone thinks."

My mother had been standing slightly crouched. Now she straightened and looked at me out of her wide pale eyes, grown great with some torment I would never understand. If I was a man, weak, she was a woman with a power in her not a woman's.

"From the beginning you were bewitched."

It was the same accusation I had made to Cecilia. I felt us all strangely connected.

"From the day she walked into this house you were a person with a mark on you, like a plague, like a cross on your forehead. On that day this day was foretold."

My father didn't like the sound of her voice. He edged toward her, but stopped as her hand made a wide sweep in his direction; it was like a magic pass, an invisible wall erected between them.

"I saw it in her," my mother went on, her voice trembling but powerful. "I recognized it, don't think I didn't! There is a kind of woman . . ."

"Now then, Nora – "

"*There is a kind of woman* . . . !" Her voice rose threateningly, and he subsided. " . . . who does not love a man, but *consumes* him." She laughed: a little half snort, part sob. "You wondered why I opposed her! I knew you would fall under her power . . . and be – engulfed. Because there's a kind of man – " her voice quivered with contempt, "who is *so easily* swallowed up."

She stood smiling bitterly, sizing me up and slowly shaking her head back and forth. My father smoothed his hair rapidly many times with his hand. I sensed that Mathilde had fled from the hall.

It occurred to me that I might say a fearful thing, and was almost relieved when she started up again . . . though what she had to say was hard to hear:

"My punishment for sending her to my sister . . . " she breathed the words out softly, " . . . was the knowledge of what my sister suffered on her account."

Well okay, they'd said it now. A mean feeling started up in me: the feeling a man must have when he murders.

"Love," she said passionately, "love is good, love ennobles and inspires! But *this* – "

"What about this?" I said, full of spite. "What you're doing, do you call this love? It doesn't make me feel ennobled!"

"There's a terrible look in your eyes," she whispered, drawing back. I thought the same about her. "A look of evil . . . " And she too, as she stared, her face transfixed, her pupils shrunken and the whites of her eyes large and glittering; they were not her eyes at all. "I wouldn't know you," she whimpered, "you're like – somebody else."

I felt it in me, loathing, and a most awful desire, related to love but an opposite feeling. It was no mere absence of love, but a will to the destruction of love. She saw it in me, while I felt it in myself and observed it in her. Around us in the air it had existence, combatting the joy which possessed the atmosphere by natural right.

The next minute she broke into tears. My father started toward her, but she waved him violently away.

The bond was between her and me, a bond of hatred which we ourselves had to break. I seemed to be down in a great depth, and she was looking at me in this depth, as though down a well. Her tears, flowing freely, seemed almost to fall on me. I looked at her, at her face puckered and tormented, and I felt her tears. I was touched by her grief and lifted up. I entered into her experience, and found myself closer to her than I had ever been to anyone, except to Cecilia in love, and perhaps equally with that. Passion and compassion: two sides of the same thing.

"Mother," I said. "Mother." I reached out and touched her and she moved quickly into my arms and clung to me like a child. I held her tenderly, full of sorrow, and something so painful it could be love.

Then my father came to our side.

"Together now . . . " he drew a long breath, "we shall recover our sense of proportion, and make our way back to reason." I looked at him and saw the muscles around his mouth contort a little and then grow firm. "Reason," he said, with great control and great passion, "can always . . . be made to prevail."

The strength of a man, I thought suddenly, shows in his mouth.

Things moved swiftly. Now there was going to be a dinner at Woehill House. The Doctor would be there, and the Professor.

"Both together?" I asked my father.

"Why shouldn't they come together?"

"Well, they never have, not at the dinner table. They're so different."

"There has to be a way of bridging differences, Hedleigh," he said. "We have been too separate here."

Cecilia was to come and bring her friend. "The Indian," he said, smiling in a nice way, "who is not our kind. Perhaps we shall find in the end that we are all the same kind."

"What is this," I said, "a council of war?"

He answered, "A council of peace."

134

"It won't do any good," I told him. "Cecilia isn't open to reason."

I had let slip the proposition I'd made her, that if she would live in Vancouver I'd consent to go to University. Heaven and earth were now to be turned in the service of persuasion.

I didn't explain to her the purpose of the dinner when inviting her; but by the way she smiled I thought she knew. She always saw the Idea behind any strategy. And this one was fairly obvious. Now that they might lose me altogether, they were willing to compromise: it was that simple.

But it would not be so simple for them to put the plan into effect. I was almost curious to see them try. They would not be approaching an ordinary human weakness in Cecilia, whom I had considered impervious to any influence but her own. They would be dealing, I decided, with a fatal flaw.

The how-do-you-do's held a note of hope. There was purpose in the air. But what when every purpose is different? I stood to one side, awkward in my tie and dark suit, and wondered at the Idea behind this. Could there be, as Cecilia had hinted, another purpose underlying them all, which synthesized them in some way?

I experienced a slight shock when confronted with the strange Eastern woman, Madame Bashir. Her face was so different from any I had known, earth brown and powerfully moulded, intense and at the same time calm. Her black eyes looked into me as though I were of a great depth and immensely interesting. I was tongue-tied and glad of my father's finesse:

"It was so very kind of you to come, Madame Bashir."

"I could not have done otherwise."

135

A strange dignity hung over the proceedings.

"Please meet our good friend, Doctor Holtzman."

They were an odd pair, strong and original looking, similar in that, yet so opposite: she the mystic, and he the scientific man of medicine. Yet fleetingly I recalled his crystalline flights of speculation . . . and hadn't Cecilia used the words "occult science"?

The Professor was all dressed up: he had had his suit pressed and somehow managed to get the ink off his fingers. He looked at Madame Bashir as though she were an unclassified specimen from antiquity. She smiled upon him as a brother.

Flowers were everywhere. There might have been a wedding or a funeral going on. The latter, you'd have thought, from the look of Mathilde as she took the coats. But Cecilia was dressed like a bride. Her white dress touched the floor and was draped somewhat like a sari. With her black hair done up in a coil, and her skin toasted a deep gold from the summer, she could have been a daughter to Madame Bashir.

Strangely, while Cecilia had put up her hair, my mother had changed the style of years, and her hair tonight fell softly about her face. She had cut it – I hadn't noticed until I saw them together. She was probably trying to look younger. From across the living room she did; she looked like a girl, lovely in a gown of yellow lace.

My father passed me by with the cocktails, but pressed a sherry on me; I took it down in gulps to get it over with. The deep blue of the living room walls began to turn translucent.

Extra lamps had been brought in; and the light shone into the upper reaches, which usually were shadowy because of the height. I noticed how beautiful were the proportions of the room. Proportion: my father's favourite subject. Proportion was the name of the evening.

They had always talked of gracious living, and I'd never been able to see it. Now for some reason I caught the Idea. I felt the piercing loveliness of the surroundings and heard with pleasure the tender tones and rippling laughter. How fine it all was: the graceful gesture, the elegant turn of a head; people at their best with each other, charming, attentive and gay. In a world of ugliness and pain, here was respite. Could it not even be, as my father believed, our duty to make a clearing in the woods, we who could? I watched him admiringly as he moved about attending to drinks, to the flow of talk, and to my mother's ease. Her eyes lifted to him with gratitude and respect. He was so relaxed in his dinner jacket, he might have been born in it; and the Doctor too wore his as comfortably as his fishing garb.

The ladies looked the eternal feminine amid a pride of men. Madame Bashir was ablaze in a cerise sari trimmed with gold; gold earrings swung gently at each stately move of her head. Several times I found her eyes fixed on me; they seemed almost to smile, though her mouth was solemnly pursed. When she raised her sherry glass to her lips, it was with the sacramental air of a temple celebrant.

My father had seated himself beside her on the Victorian sofa, and by the few words I could catch I knew he was asking her about her work with Cecilia. He queried something, and I heard her say calmly and with confidence, "Life happens. And death. It is better to understand."

What did she mean? Didn't she know that no one has ever been able to understand life and death?

My father seemed to feel he was needed across the room. As he stood Cecilia got up too and came over to me; I smiled up at her, but she wasn't looking. She simply took me by the hand and led me to where the woman sat.

"What do you think of him, Madame Bashir?" she asked, as though I were something under glass. She emphasized the second syllable of the name: Ba-*sheer*. We were all crowded onto the narrow sofa with her. I smelt a strange perfume, incense or something.

"I think he is old." The pronouncement was made with finality, with a look of friendliness, almost of complicity.

"Eighteen next January," I said, wondering. Was she pulling my leg or what? It probably didn't sound very old to her. She was maybe forty.

"He wishes, Madame Bashir . . . " Cecilia laughed, but her voice was respectful, "you'd call a spade a spade."

"Oh yes?" The woman went on, speaking quickly and with great animation. "But a spade is wood also, and metal, and these have been in existence long before they took the shape of a spade. So although we call the instrument a spade, if we look past the name we will see it as something more. Perhaps?" With this word was a quick, brilliant smile.

"Yes, I guess so," I mumbled and reached for some peanuts.

Dinner was announced in a surly fashion by Mathilde, who had not deigned to change out of her everyday dress. She had fussed with the dinner and the house as a mark of respect for the occasion; but she herself was testimony to her disrespect of the central guest. She did not look at Madame Bashir as we filed past her across the hall and into the dining room, my mother and the Doctor leading the way. My father had offered his arm to Madame, and they followed, incongruous as they were together. He stooped a little now and she carried her head like a queen, appearing to soar above him.

I had hoped to take Cecilia in, but the Professor got her first, probably by pre-arrangement with my parents. So I trailed in last, alone. The dining room looked on fire from the candlelight. Mathilde appeared to have hauled out the entire family cache of silver; tiered candelabras stood all along the sideboard and on the various small tables around the walls. The walnut panelling that reached halfway up the room reflected the flickering lights in a golden blur. It was as though the walls swam in gentle movement. And the candles set aglow the fabric on the upper walls, which once had been a deep warm red, embossed with velvet blooms, but was now the colour of burnt-out roses. I noted the contrast between the old faded colours and the fresh flowers in the centre of the table, with their true and brilliant hues, heightened still more by the shaft of white light from the chandelier above them.

The room smelt of fresh wax and rain. It had been teeming all afternoon, and Mathilde had thrown open the french windows while she waxed the woodwork. The dinner she had had in hand for a week. "Mathilde," my father had teased her, "it's not the dog you are putting on for our guest of honour, it's the sacred cow." She was not amused.

She hoped, like my parents, that the oracle could be persuaded to keep Cecilia in the West and me in their sight. But her attitude was one of invincible superiority. The fine pieces around us were intended to show how very much better we were, how unattainably separate and removed. (Or is that what they always are for?)

We were shown our places at the table, not the usual oval with my parents at either end, distinguished by position, but perfectly circular tonight, with its central leaf inserted. I knew better than to hope Cecilia would be beside me, and they didn't put her across from me either, where I could look at her. They placed her strategically around the curve on the other side of the Professor, who was at my left. I could only see her by turning away from my mother on my right. Beyond my mother was the Doctor, then Madame Bashir and my father.

Madame Bashir looked around and said, beaming, "We are seven at the table. It's a good sign."

There was an awful silence. Into it rushed my mother. "Eight, with Mathilde!" And she laughed. Mathilde was leaning between her and me, digging us both with her elbows, putting the fresh bread on the table. "Mathilde is one of the family."

"To be sure," said Madame. "We are all one of the family." She threw a brilliant smile at Mathilde, who scowled. That would have made them sisters.

I was struck with an odd feeling: the round table, the candlelight swaying at our backs and catching the crown of hair on those across from us, across the white table all gleaming with glass and old metal. I felt we had all been here before, exactly like this.

I looked out the window. The long plum-coloured drapes at the french windows had been left undrawn; my mother always said the room was so effective at night, reflected in the glass. I gazed at us all out there above the water, with the night sky above and below us, and felt that that was more real, more enduring, than this. Those people silently laughing and talking could not be destroyed by calamity or time or even by each other. Though they seemed stationed in darkness they fed upon the light at the centre of the stars, and, sustained by love, lived forever.

My mother's look was resting on me, tender and sad. "I sometimes wonder," she said in a low voice, "if Mathilde may have been right, and we should sometimes have had a blessing at this table."

"Not her kind," I said jocularly, hoping to dispel her seriousness before it got serious. "All full of petitions and mourning for our sins."

"To be able to acknowledge our sins," she murmured, "may be the highest blessing of all."

Did she mean mine? No, for she smiled and touched my hand.

"Now enjoy your dinner. Mathilde has surpassed herself."

That was evident by the way my father was holding the edges of the soup plates with her over there as she set them down. We were getting Mathilde's Absolute Specialty, chestnut soup with cognac. When the occasion was inordinately special, the brew called for extra tasting, with the result that the cook was ever so slightly tipsy when she came to serve it. There had never been such a special dinner as this at Woehill House, with so much at stake.

And now my father took the conversation by the horns. Raising his wine glass he turned to Madame Bashir and said in his most courtly manner:

"We are honoured that East and West meet here tonight. Let us drink to unity."

All drank, while Cecilia said flatly: "East is outnumbered."

"That's a switch." The Doctor turned to Madame Bashir and grinned. "I guess you've solved your birth control problem at last," he said, then amended hastily: "Speaking generally of course."

Everyone laughed, in varying shades of nervousness, she herself with genuine delight.

The Professor threw an oblique look at me and began: "Past and future meet also . . . "

He was going to make a speech, I could tell. I said quickly, "So here's to the present."

"Ah, but the present is fleeting," he intoned and looked vaguely around. "Do you not think so?"

"I do." Promptly, from Madame Bashir. "The present is everything, and everything is fleeting."

I glanced past the Professor at Cecilia. A little smile lit her face.

My mother decided it was time to normalize things.

"How long have you been in this country, Madame Ba-shir?" she asked.

"I was born here."

"What?" Mathilde chimed in from the background. "You're Canadian?" She sounded horrified.

Madame turned around in her chair and smiled at her. "I am. But I'm sorry to say my parents were prejudiced, so I was sent to India for my schooling."

Firm ground at last, and the Professor jumped happily up and down on it. "Ah yes, yes, indeed yes. Education makes the person. It always goes back to that."

Almost inaudibly Madame murmured, "And perhaps further back."

"Prenatal influence, do you mean?" the Doctor asked, giving her a curious look.

"She meant further still," said Cecilia.

The image of a spade came into my mind: materials older than form, and I said suddenly, "Oh. Reincarnation!"

Mathilde sent a wine glass sprawling. My father snatched up his table napkin and started dabbing, while my mother kept up a running series of "Oh dears." The Professor stayed bent over his soup.

"Well now, Madame Bashir!" the Doctor's voice rose over the commotion, eager and perhaps slightly mocking. "You must straighten me out on one or two points . . ."

My father turned to the right and began a patter of talk with Cecilia, who kept her eyes on her plate and occasionally nodded. My mother too was full of sweet nothings, bending my ear in her direction, preventing me from hearing what the Doctor and Madame Bashir were saying. I watched my father break skilfully into their talk.

"But surely," I heard him say to Madame, "we need our illusions."

"I do not think so." She smiled, but her tone was serious.

"O'Neill in *The Iceman Cometh*, shows that our illusions enable us to endure reality."

"It may have been the only way O'Neill could endure it. That does not establish a law."

"She's right, Gerry." The Doctor leaned round her to my father, who hated to be called Gerry. It was one of his illusions that the use of the name Gerald preserved his identity.

My mother had fallen silent, probably with shock. It was extremely bad form to insist upon a point at dinner, or even make one, particularly if you were a woman; most particularly a woman talking to a man. And when the man was your host. . . !

At last I could hear what was happening.

"Illusion is useful," Madame said, "only inasmuch as it leads us toward more endurable realities. Once we have contacted these, we can cast off illusion."

"And how do we know," my father inquired studiously, "when these have been contacted?"

"We may not always know how," she said firmly, "but we know."

I thought with amazement, she sounds like Cecilia!

The Doctor looked thoughtful. Mathilde was now busy whipping the soup plates out from before us, empty or not. She was probably going to drain them in the kitchen, along with the wine glasses.

A few minutes later she came back in, bearing the roast beef aloft on a platter as though it were an imperial crown. She wheeled round toward the table with such panache that my father leaped out of his chair and, gently smiling, relieved her of it.

He kept the conversation general while he carved, but soon lost Madame again to the Doctor. So he redoubled his efforts on Cecilia, and my mother on me, while the Professor kept his head swivelling back and forth between us as extra fortification. I would have loved to eat in silence; but in polite company no terror was greater.

Did politeness, I wondered, consist merely in warding off fear? I remembered that we were sitting directly above the caves, home of the Jotuns; you'd almost think we had formed a charmed circle to keep from falling into them, and were holding ourselves up by a type of gas generated in the larynx.

My ears took in the low thrum of the Doctor's and Madame Bashir's conversation. It had struck a slightly higher vibratory note, though their voices were pitched low.

Mathilde was the only one who could hear everything, as she slowly circled the table behind us, purporting to keep an eye on our wine and water glasses. I could see that she was determined not to miss a word, and I kept drinking up my water to oblige her; I had to excuse myself finally, and she had grown so mellow she showed me out as though I didn't know the direction. For an awful minute I thought she was going to stay with me all the way. But back she trotted, with her mouth pulled in and her ears sticking out.

As I rejoined them, I glanced around the Professor at Cecilia, and fancied she threw me a fast wink. I grinned at her, but saw her face then solemn and forbidding, and decided I must have been mistaken.

Suddenly a word rose up out of the Doctor's and Madame's conversation:

" . . . Shiva . . . "

It created a pall around the table. She continued animatedly, "Lord Shiva. One of the three faces of God. In the West you have a Creator . . ." she laughed, "when you have anything. We see the Creator as containing within Himself – and Herself – two others: the Preserver, who preserves what is created, and Lord Shiva the Destroyer, who destructs the old forms when they have served their usefulness, so that new ones may arise."

"But this force," the Doctor said, "exists everywhere."

"Certainly. Here it's called autumn . . . or the devil."

"Or the Angel of Death, by God!" the Doctor said. "My mortal enemy."

"Do you not think," she remarked, "that sometimes we wrestle with him too hard? He's not so much to be feared."

The Doctor gave a grunt. "Try telling that to my patients."

I became aware of my mother staring past me. She was looking at Cecilia with an air of recognition. I turned to Cecilia. Her look too was of something stirring in the depths. In my own mind remembrance flickered. I saw the shower of broken china falling round her, and heard her scathing voice as I had heard it always, attacking and questioning, burning with scorn the old, the dried-up, institutions.

I asked in the silence, "But don't the forces of preservation and destruction clash?"

"Continually!" Madame Bashir looked across at me, pleased. "Their clash is what makes the world go round."

"I thought that was love!" My father spoke playfully, making light of it all.

"It is!" She sounded delighted. "The true labour of love. The tussle that makes for progress." She went on rapidly, speaking with vigour, almost with joy. "Progress consists of creating new forms: step one. These must be preserved: step two. But they are allowed to endure only so long. If they are clung to beyond a certain point they become part of the backward drift. What was good starts to go bad. Therefore, step three: destruction."

And now her features seemed to soften. Her voice was tender as she said, looking not quite at but just past my father. "This last often happens painfully and with a struggle. It wasn't meant to be that way. And it wouldn't be, if a balance could be struck. It's all a question of proportion."

Balance and proportion: his own great theme. I watched him curiously. His face was quite pink: it may have been the wine. And in his eyes I seemed to see a struggle going on, a clash perhaps between two of the faces of God, where one had possessed him solely until now . . . with his consent but without his knowledge.

During dessert, as the talk went on around me, I contemplated Cecilia's mysterious involvement with this teacher. I saw that she was reaching for a stratum of knowledge existing beyond the boundaries of what is acceptable in our time and place; that she had ventured over that boundary; and I could neither keep pace with her nor call her back.

Then we were finished. The table was a ruin. As we stood, I glanced through the window at the company out over the sea. They rose as we did, but were graced by silence, and left no devastation behind them. They turned and moved through space, toward freedom, while we headed for the living room where The Issue would soon be raised and was already filling me with dread.

We found the cups set out, and coffee steaming on the heater in its silver well. The room looked different to me than it had before: artificial and too formal. Everything was stationed around in a deliberate pose, as though planning a deception. The windows were uncovered in here too, for the night effect which my mother always loved, though not tonight.

It was Madame Bashir who stood spellbound at the sight of the full moon hanging low over the water. It had a serenity which matched her own. She didn't take her eyes from it as she went slowly to a chair and sat. Full moon: witch's night. I felt that if I were to look away and not too quickly back, I might see her with the moon in her lap.

My mother poured the coffee. Her social chatter was used up, and she was pale and silent. When everyone was neatly balancing a little cup and saucer, my father leaned forward and began, "How fine it is when friends can assemble in this way. This drawing together is after all the central purpose of living. At least I can think of no other more important. Oh, Frank . . . " He turned attentively to Doctor Holtzman. "Have you cream?" The Doctor liked cream with his after-dinner coffee, even though it was declassé.

"You bet. Go ahead with what you're saying. What *are* you saying anyway?"

"I'm saying it's nice to have you here."

"You've been saying that for eighteen years. Are you saying you mean it, is that what you're saying?"

"That's about the size of it," my father laughed, then went on quickly, "Yes, it was – just eighteen years ago – that you first came to see us. Or to see Nora, rather. For Hedleigh was on the way."

On the way! I was disgusted. He made it sound as though I were journeying by train, or stork, or something. I didn't dare look at Cecilia.

"We were a little concerned," my father went on in a tender tone. "She wasn't strong."

She wasn't? Why, seeing her gardening, you'd think she was strong as a horse. I sneaked a look at her. She was gazing modestly down at her hands, like a speaker about to be introduced.

"I don't remember that part," Holtzman said, "but never mind."

My father put down his cup and groped uneasily in a pocket for his pipe.

"Why yes, that was the reason she didn't have more children. When there are other children, the loss of one is not quite so catastrophic."

147

Now they were talking as though I'd died. The Professor turned slowly and looked at me, to reassure himself I was still there. Madame Bashir was smiling placidly out at the moon.

"The loss of . . . who? What're you talking about?" asked the Doctor in a baffled tone.

"I was merely intending to say . . . " my father was stuffing his pipe and getting his bearings, "that I hope we – all of us – this very seven – " his eyes rested with particular warmth upon Cecilia "can meet like this often again." He paused briefly. "If it is so fated." He cast a charming smile at Madame Bashir, who simultaneously redirected her attention from the moon and smiled broadly back at him. "As to whether or not there is anything in the concept of fate, who can say?" he went on. "These are things we cannot ever know. But be that as it may . . . "

Buoyed up with optimism, I put in my two cents' worth. "The Valkyrs refer to the Choosers of the Slain," I explained importantly to the room. "They believed that an immutable destiny appointed which of them would be killed."

"I rather think, Hedleigh," my father snapped, "that we might do without historical statements at this time!"

I retired from the floor; but I was burning. So this is what my years of application to History had come to!

My father's composure was gone. He packed his pipe rapidly, shedding tobacco all down his front, a thing he never did. Everyone waited, while his first half-dozen matches went out. He stood up and turned his back to the window, shielding himself from an imaginary draft. I looked past him at the others out there, patiently sitting, and wondered just what they were waiting for.

Finally he had it lit, and puffed away for a moment before tackling the thing again, this time on his feet.

"Now I'm going to make an appeal to reason here to-night!" As he spoke he slowly pivoted, his eyes earnestly seeking out each face. "People are fond of specifying the one characteristic that separates man from lower forms of life. I myself think it is reason. Do you agree, by any chance, Madame Bashir?" He came to rest confronting her, like a roulette wheel ceasing at the whim of chance.

"I do agree," she answered, with a small gracious dip of her head.

"Ah!"

" . . . that reason separates man from lower and also from higher forms of life."

"Higher?" He was stumped.

She resumed her contemplation of the moon.

"Ah yes, higher. Yes, I see." He sounded nervous and slightly appeasing. "Higher, you mean the nobler, more generous impulses in people – which are beyond reason certainly. They occur of their own accord if they are going to, if they are in us." He shot a brief, significant glance at me. "Although it may be reasonable to suppose that these most frequently exist in a rationally minded person."

The words spilled from his lips like beads off a broken string and seemed to hit the floor. The Doctor was having trouble concentrating; he shifted in his chair and rubbed an eye from time to time.

"I am sure, at any rate," my father went on, effusively, "that where there is good will, reason can and shall prevail."

"And where there is good reason . . . " Madame's head turned slowly to him "you may find that will prevails."

There was a power in her words, or in her manner of saying them. Cecilia was watching her, sitting very straight, with her head held high in the same way, though that had always been her own way too. I wondered suddenly what her mother had been like. And only then did it dawn on me that this woman was some sort of mother to her.

My father passed over her remark and turned to the Doctor, saying in an amiable way:

"I don't know, Frank, whether you knew that our Cecilia wants to go away and study Art."

Our Cecilia! I bent over my cold coffee, humiliated for him.

"She's thinking of going to Montreal," he continued blandly. "We think it rather a long way from home."

From "home." I couldn't bear it. I put down my cup and tore at my hair; my feet got itchy, and only a sharp glance from my father set me still. I stared at my hands and wished I were dead.

"Cecilia and Hedleigh are very . . . attached. Any move she might make will affect him too. And, consequently, us; though that is not the prime . . . " He had the grace to falter.

My mother was watching him intently, with an air almost of supplication, as a prisoner in the dock might watch the defending counsel. The judge here was Madame Bashir, and accordingly kept herself aloof from the proceedings, stepping down only now and then for a brief pontification. Right now she was gazing past my father's head, attentive, but rather less to him than to something in the air around him.

"We are concerned here not with a single event but with a life. Two lives," he added just in time. He took up a position before the window, like an actor moving into the spotlight for an important soliloquy. "If youth only knew that its snap decisions become the long, lingering years of age. Many are the souls who have wept throughout those years with the memory of early aspiration, and have gone to their graves still haunted by what might have been."

I decided then and there not to be a writer. There was

something shameful about words: you could twist them like a handful of snakes, charm them into all the directions in which people manipulate other people.

As though to prove it, my mother leaned forward and said with gentle concern:

"How do you plan to keep yourself in Montreal, Cecilia? It costs a lot of money . . . "

"My board and schooling have been arranged," Cecilia said with perfect equanimity, though if you knew her well you could detect a tautness in her.

"Oh yes." My mother spoke with an air of knowing. She was about to go on, but my father broke in with great heartiness:

"Yes, naturally, Cecilia will be looked after by her family. I mean to contribute to her maintenance myself, wherever she is . . . as I have done here." He cast a sideways look at my mother; he was not pleased with her.

But her question had revived a suspicion, buried alive in my mind. I was already picturing our Uncle Frederick paying a visit to Montreal . . . I turned a cold look on my mother.

"But now Cecilia, my dear." My father produced a warm smile and walked over to her, his countenance light and innocent. "I want to ask you one simple question: Why must it be Montreal?"

Her face closed over. She glanced quickly at Madame Bashir. I followed her look and saw that lady deeply absorbed in the spectacle of her cerise-draped knees.

"I know Montreal is thought to be the art centre of Canada." My father's tone was gently derogatory. "But that is a matter of opinion. And in any case, does a student need a whole art centre? Sometimes one good teacher. . . ." He turned back with a gesture to Madame. "You found Madame Bashir in Vancouver. . . . "

Cecilia looked small and alone in the big wing chair; I

wished this prize teacher would come to her aid. My father bent over her, his hand on the back of the chair. She stared at the buttons of his coat. "If you stay here, he'll go to University! Cecilia . . . please understand . . . " He was pleading with her now: it was pathetic. "It's not that we want to hang onto him. It's that we want him to make something of himself."

Her head flew up. She said in clear, brave voice, "I think he's something already."

He straightened at this riposte, while I stared at her, overcome with flattery and a hopeless hope.

My father puffed quickly on his pipe and glanced at my mother for support. But she had sunk back into a corner of the sofa and wore a look of listless despair.

The Doctor, however, was chipper, his face alive with interest, and his eyes sweeping the faces around him like a searchlight seeking out a wreck.

"I mean to say, Cecilia," my father drove on gamely, "we are greatly concerned for Hedleigh's education."

"Oh yes, that," she said flatly. It was all she'd ever heard about since she came into the house at the age of twelve.

If anybody in this world had educated me, she had. I wished I had the courage to stand up and say so.

Then suddenly, there I was, standing in the middle of the room; it was as though I'd leaped a gap in time. I had said it. And with fervour. The faces turned to me were of a wonderful variety, from my father's, which looked frozen, to Madame Bashir's, tilted up and bright with ap-probation. Cecilia had sat back into the chair, her spine relaxed, and was looking around the room with a merry smile. The Professor shakily set down his cup and saucer; he didn't know what had happened.

My mother sat up from her corner and started plucking at the neck of her dress as though something were choking her. My father looked over at her with ostentatious concern, then said to me softly, "Cecilia may just possibly have omitted lessons in charity."

No, charity wasn't what you might call Cecilia's strong point. I answered him reasonably and calmly, "I didn't say my education was complete. I only said where I got it from." Oh damn. Preposition.

"Okay, Gerry!" The Doctor leaned forward, arms folded on his knees. "What've you got to say to that?"

"Let us hear from Madame Bashir," countered my father. "I should be interested in her viewpoint on Cecilia going East." He made her a slight bow. "Perhaps I should say to the near East."

He earned one of her quick, brilliant smiles. She said merely, "I have already made my view known to Cecilia." And she lifted her eyes again to the moon, gazing fixedly, as though into a great crystal ball.

"Ah yes." My father resumed gingerly. "I am aware that certain methods exist . . . by which it is deemed possible to foretell the future. For myself, I have always eschewed anything less than the free will of man."

"A man on a journey," she said to the moon, "can freely decide whether or not to study a road map."

"Ah," he responded softly, with a note of triumph. "But who is to say where the road map is kept?"

She spread open one hand. "Perhaps we carry it in our glove compartment."

They watched each other. I looked around furtively at the others. The Professor's face wore the blank look of a student who has blundered into the wrong class. My mother was carefully smoothing a white lace handkerchief on her lap.

My father spoke briskly. "Well, to be practical. Montreal is a French milieu, after all. As an American, Cecilia will always be happier in the West."

Madame Bashir raised her hand in a slow, emphatic

movement: the judge pronouncing her *res judicata.* "That . . . is for Cecilia to discover."

My mother's lace handkerchief fluttered to the floor. The Professor, who was nearest to her, stood creakingly and bent his long body to pick it up. He remained there holding it in his hand, which was trembling a little, and he looked like someone waving a white flag.

"That may be," said my father, "but it's within our province, we who hold a longer view, to divert heartbreak when we see it imminent."

Madame Bashir drew her sari around her with a graceful, definite movement, as she said, "Heartbreak is a flowing river that will not be diverted."

"Well, you don't have to jump into it!" My father was losing patience.

Her smile appeared again out of nowhere.

"No!" She gathered in a stray end of her robe. "But in a certain season, when the weather indicates that it might overflow its banks, it may be necessary to go forth to meet it."

"Perhaps," my father said with desperate courtesy, "if we could restore the conversation to firm ground, and be a little less aquatic . . . "

"I don't know!" Holtzman interrupted with verve. "When you're dealing with bathers the water's damn significant."

My father glared at him. I wanted to laugh. The thing was getting rather joyous.

"The bathing habits of early Mesarabians . . . " Gladsomely the Professor joined the stream, "notwithstanding the grave threat of crocodiles . . . "

"Edgar!" My father turned to him. *"Would you mind?"*

I absolutely couldn't help it: a laugh rose up and I turned it into a tremendous cough. I saw a sudden movement to the right of me and glanced at Cecilia and looked quickly away, lest I die. She too had the giggles. Holding a handkerchief to her mouth, she looked as though she might have a fishbone stuck in her throat.

Doctor Holtzman got up (had he seen our predicament?) and paced back and forth making a great stir with his hands.

"Now I think this river business is interesting, and I'd like to hear more about it." He bowed toward the Professor, who was blinking in bewilderment. "And about Mesarabia too – some other time." He cleared his throat with a rumble. He was perhaps having the same trouble as we were. Altogether the sound in the room was that of a rhino herd with the flu. Mathilde, who I knew could not be far outside the living room door, must have been glad of the chance to shift her position and get a good hold on her beads.

Doctor Holtzman turned to my father.

"You mentioned heartbreak. My work brings me in contact with heartbreak all the time. This is something the human animal has never learned to cope with."

I was dizzy from fighting my laughter, and from the heat, which seemed to be increasing in the room. I looked longingly at the people outside above the cool water. Behind me the Doctor's voice went on, "Of one thing I am convinced. We lay too much store by the pleasure principle. We're so busy chasing after the pleasure and away from the pain, we're missing the joy."

The moon shed its great light upon the others. They sat in the direct path of the light which did not reach us, confined as we were within walls; and they were very still, still and cool, entirely detached and serene. Not a hair of their heads stirred in the wind that was rising.

The wind seemed to shake the voice of the Doctor as he asked, "What are we for? What are we made for anyway? I'll tell you what I think we're made for, and I'm convinced

of it! We're made for happiness! We're designed for joy
. . . to experience, create and communicate joy!"

Behind me, out of my sight, was Cecilia who had
created joy for me. The girl on the edge of the group before
me sat very still. It was something new for her to have
people wanting to keep her, she who had always been
driven out and away . . . by herself. . . .

To herself! The thought moved forward from where it
was already present in my mind.

"You don't understand!" My mother's voice erupted behind me. "Hedleigh is going to follow her to Montreal!"

"So let him!" The Doctor's voice overlapped her. "Help
him pack!"

I could feel the thumping of my heart, but the boy out
there, who resembled me, looked in possession of himself.
He told me with one look from his eyes why I lost the joy
whenever Cecilia went out of my sight. It was because I
hadn't made it for myself. And I hadn't created any for her;
I'd only given her back her own joy, warmed up.

I took a few steps toward the window, separating myself from the argument building behind me. The Doctor
was saying that a man needs two women, one to give him
life and one to sustain it. "The creator, you might say, and
the preserver. The destroyer he can do without." It was a
private set-to between the Doctor and my mother; I felt I
shouldn't turn around – especially when her tears began to
fall.

There was the same space between them and me as
between me and the others out there: an impassable gulf.

The argument went on. My mind seemed to fall away
from them and from what they were saying, and as it did
it approached the meaning of what they were saying; and
I saw that the will behind their words was the same.

The Doctor said finally, in pained exasperation, "Nora,
I wish to God there was something I could give you for that

heartburn!" She began to speak but he interrupted, "That's what you're suffering from, it's heartburn, a type that arises from a particular malfunction of the heart! It's very prevalent among those who . . . love."

The hesitation told me what I wanted to know. That was all that divided us – a hesitation. Their voices rose and dimmed and blurred. But my head was clearing. I knew one thing. I knew what I wanted. It was to bridge the hesitation between myself and the Others.

The voices in the room had all stopped: I didn't know how long ago.

In our silence we matched for the first time the group beyond the window. Then one of them rose, a long thin figure.

"Please . . ."

It was a piteous voice from behind me. I turned and saw the Professor, gray and ghostlike, extending a feeble hand in a halt sign. His mouth was slack and his chin trembled a little.

"Please, if I might be excused. . . ."

He seemed to be trying to command his feet to move. I looked at them, and at his terrified face, and saw that between his warm feet and cool brain there was a gap, like a break in an electric wire. Under stress, nothing travelled along the line at all.

He finally got himself going, stumbling toward the door, holding onto the backs of chairs. A smell of books wafted past me. Or perhaps it was the scent of books to come.

My father, who seemed also to have been deeply stilled, recovered and lunged to his side. He supported him gently, leading him along.

"Edgar, forgive me, I should have realized. You're accustomed to an early bed. I'll drive you home at once!"

They went out, and as they did Cecilia stood. She

looked fine and cool and strong as she walked toward my mother, who hovered on the edge of the group, wondering how to re-enter the lighted room. She was positioned in the vast darkness outside, and you could feel her longing.

"Would you play for us, Aunt Nora?" Cecilia asked. Her voice was young, tender and strong. She didn't wait but took my mother's hand and moved with a light step to the piano. There she whisked out the bench, turned over some music, and opened a book of old songs.

Charity. After all.

Fate hangs back, concealing its face, so that age after age its existence is argued; and more men deny it than affirm. But when it moves it moves swiftly, and if the mover is not fate, what does the name of it matter?

Cecilia's suitcases stood ready in the hall, labelled: Montreal.

I was to go to her at dusk in the studio. She was taking the night flight.

I met her between the studio and the house: she had come to meet me. We both stopped, full of staring, with no words at all. The sea foamed on the shore below us; and the sky waited for her, pouring rain. I wondered if it would hurl her down, and could almost wish it would. She would fall like a thunderbolt, leaving ruin for miles and years around. My Lady Shiva.

She took my hand and gently led me.

"Where are we going?" I asked her.

"To the tower."

We ascended slowly, quite unlike our old selves.

We stood shoulder to shoulder, facing the East through the West window. The rain streamed down before us in a silver sheet. It could not be heard where it fell: we were between its originating and its returning. Water above us and below.

There was little that could be said. I said it all:

"I love you."

She turned her face to mine in such a rush, I lost her word, or words. I thought it might be "what?"

"I love . . . " I repeated, then thought she may have asked me "who?"

Who do I love? Or who is it that loves? For if I who love am not, what does the love amount to?

All that had been gathering clicked into place. I thought fleetingly how, when the greatest things happen, they seem not to be happening; and we are used to making a furor over nothing at all.

I put my arms around her, laughing with a new and sudden joy, which my unhappiness couldn't dim. We tried wrestling, but were too close. Our arms around each other remained.

Silence up here between the two waters.

In the same silence I sit at the end of my journey. I could almost believe I haven't moved out of it, but that my life has revolved around that centre.

The sky has all but cleared during my revisiting. I needn't have been afraid. While life lived is sweet and painful both, life relived is an alchemical process which purifies the pain. Perhaps it has to do with the revealing of purpose; or is it that the humour can be seen, twinkling at last through the solemnity of old and deep involvements? They are not too deep for their time, as the inrushing sea is as full as it need be. But later when the waters draw out, and the fuss of that flux is over, there comes a peace to the edge of the land that is more in keeping with its great age.

I get up at last. My limbs are stiff, but I can look with a smile far up across the headland at the dirt road I took the night I left. I see the shadow of a boy up there, trudging along through the darkest of dark nights . . . and remember how my heart burned in my chest with the heartburn the Doctor had spoken about. It threatened to rise up and close my throat, and maybe even my resolve. Perhaps the ancient kings had such a lump, I thought, in their throats, and such a burning in the region of the heart, as they sailed away from solid land to face their ordeal by fire. But they went forward with courage, for they were men.

And perhaps, once out to sea, they made contact with the Others: with these, to whom I had made my way, and with whom I walked that night unconstrainedly through the darkness to freedom. Sadness and joy leaped the gap, the hesitation that divided the one into two, and I understood what was beyond my understanding. It came about through my pity for Mathilde, who would miss me more than my parents would. They had each other, but she, although she seemed in a way all people, seemed also only part of a person, a fragment joined always to someone else. As I had moved, she moved: I was she and she was me, but not as though we were properly united: attached, which is different.

Then I saw – Did I see it then, or was it much later? – that together is not truly together when it is attached. And separate is not alone. It's the necessary step toward union and is its other side, as isolation is the other side of attachment.

I was moved by a certainty which I could not have reasoned to my parents, or indeed anyone. I knew that the line between this area of the mind and the rational was as wide as the world. There was no way to bridge it that I could see. Yet I felt I would give all my life to be able to construct a bridge like that.

And then as I walked I wondered: have not men (real men) always, throughout history, concerned themselves with ways and means of spanning the known and the unknown, the realized and unrealized? My steps and my thought led me round in a circle, back to the dinner party, to the instant of hesitation when clearly I saw: the troubles that existed were not in things themselves, but in the gap between them, between one person and another, one generation and another, between head and heart, right and left and up and down . . . between heaven, if you like, and earth.

By the time I'd made my way to Vancouver, I was sure enough of myself to send home a postcard: "I am going to build bridges."

There is only a little cloud over the sun. I feel the warmth on my back as I approach the house . . . and start around it once, for the luck I had in it. Where the coach house was, there is space, and a new view of the hillside, the first I have seen of it. I had left Vancouver and gone East when my father wrote to say he was dismantling the building. It pained my mother to see it there, and it was no use any more, he said, it smelled of paint. It grieved me to realize they had grown bitter.

Yet I picture my father with his hand held out as though granting me forgiveness. Or perhaps I have touched self-forgiveness at last, after the long accusation. For I accepted with too little grace the bitter truth that human love is flawed. I have seen that his caring, his concern for my manhood, his noble ideals and sense of responsibility, were like a divine heritage, which I took for granted – as we take the air and sun and water, complaining more often than we worship.

And I feel my mother's face at the window, watching me from the vastness of her love. While it enclosed me, it fed me from my beginnings. My mistake was in singling out a tiny, a temporal part of it, one small eddy of disturbance to judge her by. It's as though one judged the purity and majesty of the sea by a single storm. A storm may terrify or even destroy, but the spirit of the sea is Good, taking all destruction into itself, renewing it and being renewed by it.

The sun breaks through the clouds almost as I perceive that the essential gift of love is this: to create a climate for the other's growth. This my parents did in my young years, and Cecilia later. By their behaviour toward her they provided the climate her strong soul needed for its own development. It brought them suffering, and perhaps their sacrifice was all the greater for it. I see by this light that the action of love doesn't always appear benign, and that in the end everything that happens is a form of love.

I didn't know it but I brought a problem home. Coming round again to the front door, I make a mental note to jot in my diary: "I am in debt to my parents, but my son owes me nothing." I see that that's the way it has to work to fulfil the law of love, which is an upward spiral, open at the top.

The door handle turns easily. As I step over the threshold, there is something . . . a scrap of paper or a leaf . . . which must have been lodged up above. It flutters silently onto my shoulder, like a live thing, like life left in the house.

M7